HOW TO SPOT A SASQUATCH

WRITTEN BY
J. TORRES

ILLUSTRATED BY
AURÉLIE GRAND

Owlkids Books

For my niece Kayla—

because she has big feet and even bigger ideas like, "Bigfoot could be a girl!"
— J.T.

To all the curious kids and weird creatures who wander into our lives.

And thanks to all the support from my studio team "Post-Office" in Montreal, my family, and Kim.
— A.G.

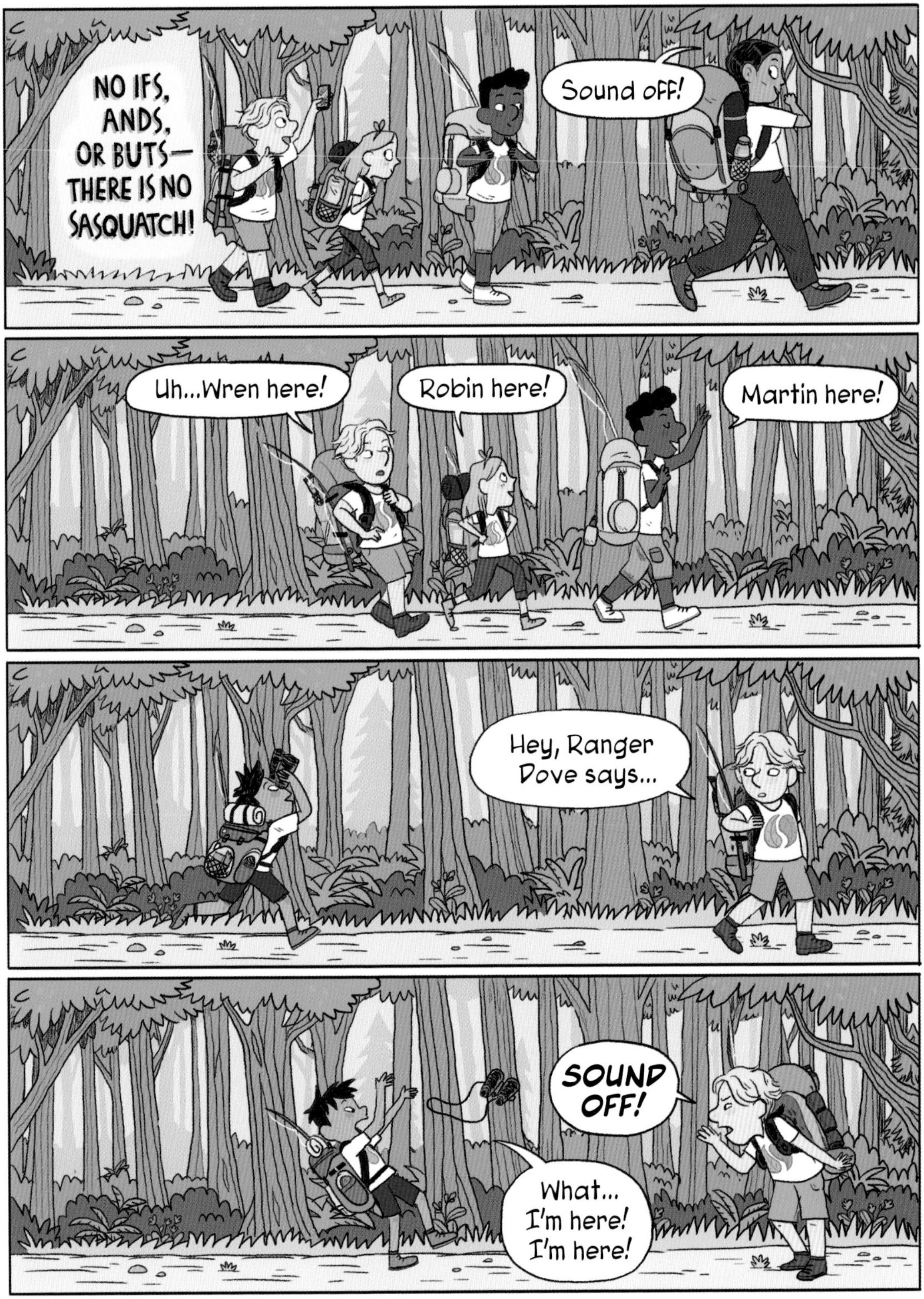
NO IFS, ANDS, OR BUTS— THERE IS NO SASQUATCH!
Sound off!
Uh...Wren here!
Robin here!
Martin here!
Hey, Ranger Dove says...
SOUND OFF!
What... I'm here! I'm here!

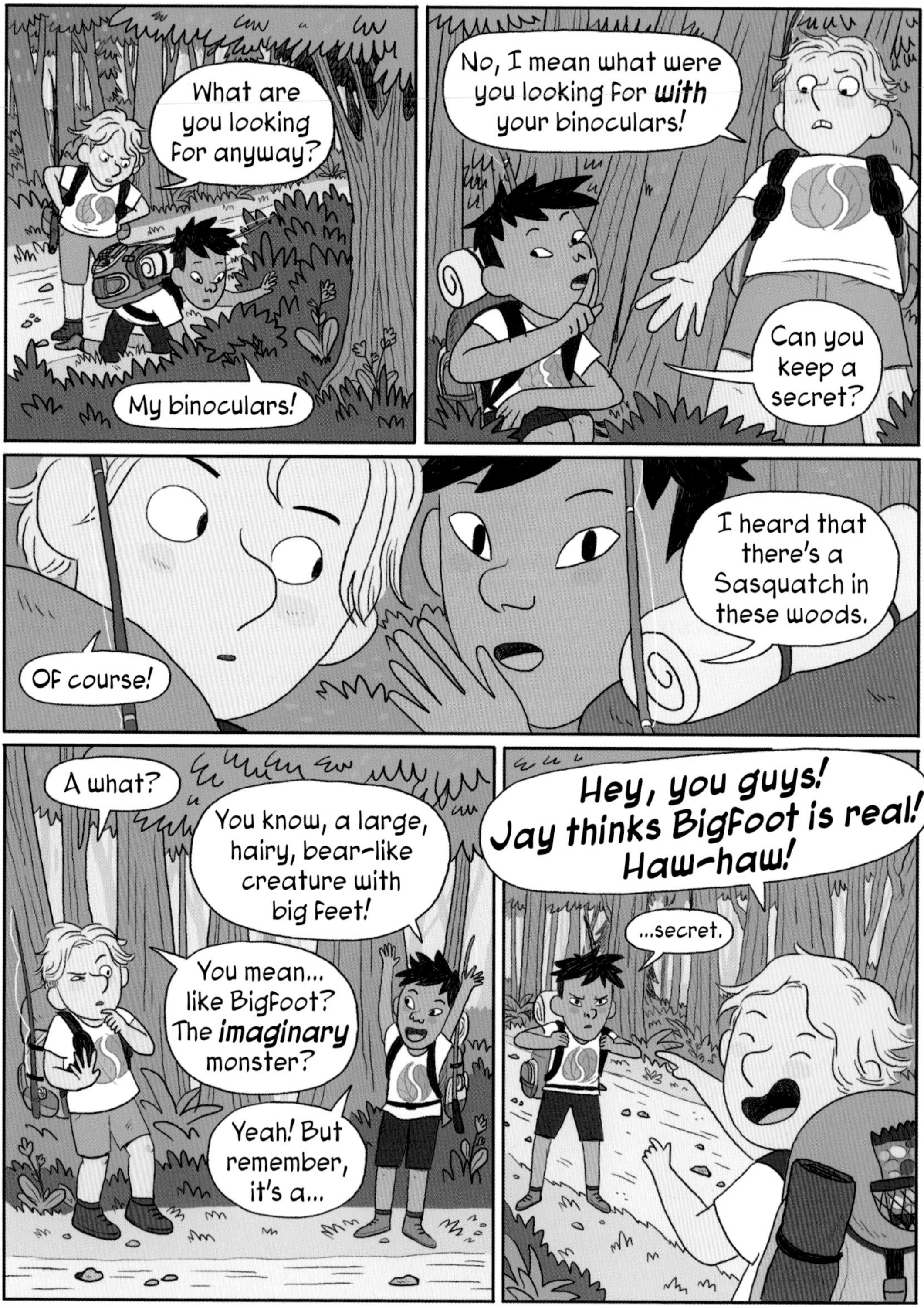
What are you looking for anyway?
My binoculars!
No, I mean what were you looking for **with** your binoculars!
Can you keep a secret?
Of course!
I heard that there's a Sasquatch in these woods.
A what?
You know, a large, hairy, bear-like creature with big feet!
You mean... like Bigfoot? The **imaginary** monster?
Yeah! But remember, it's a...
Hey, you guys! Jay thinks Bigfoot is real! Haw-haw!
...secret.

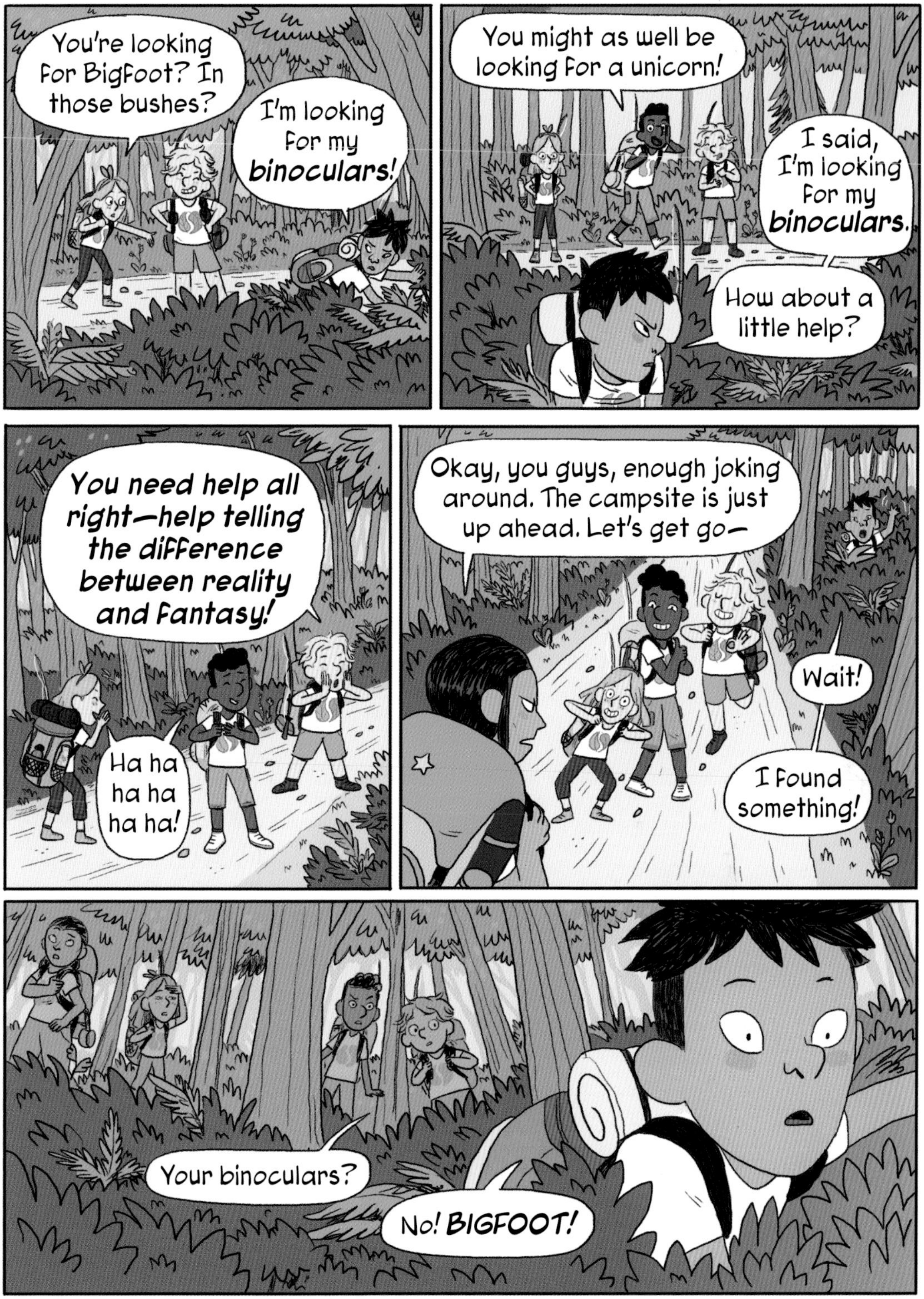
You're looking for Bigfoot? In those bushes?
I'm looking for my **binoculars!**
You might as well be looking for a unicorn!
I said, I'm looking for my **binoculars.**
How about a little help?
You need help all right—help telling the difference between reality and fantasy!
Ha ha ha ha ha ha!
Okay, you guys, enough joking around. The campsite is just up ahead. Let's get go—
Wait!
I found something!
Your binoculars?
No! **BIGFOOT!**

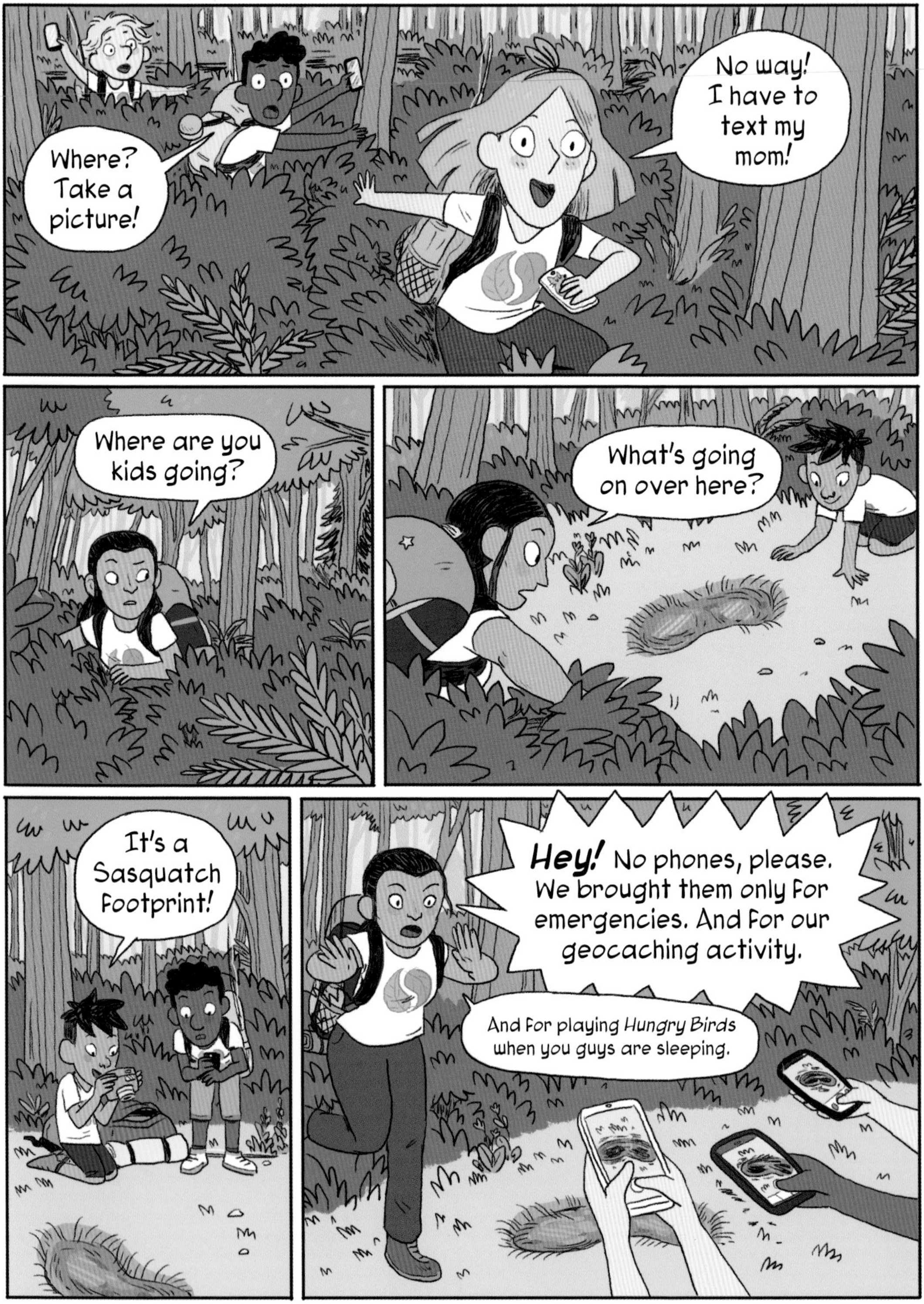
No way! I have to text my mom!
Where? Take a picture!
Where are you kids going?
What's going on over here?
It's a Sasquatch footprint!
Hey! No phones, please. We brought them only for emergencies. And for our geocaching activity.
And for playing *Hungry Birds* when you guys are sleeping.

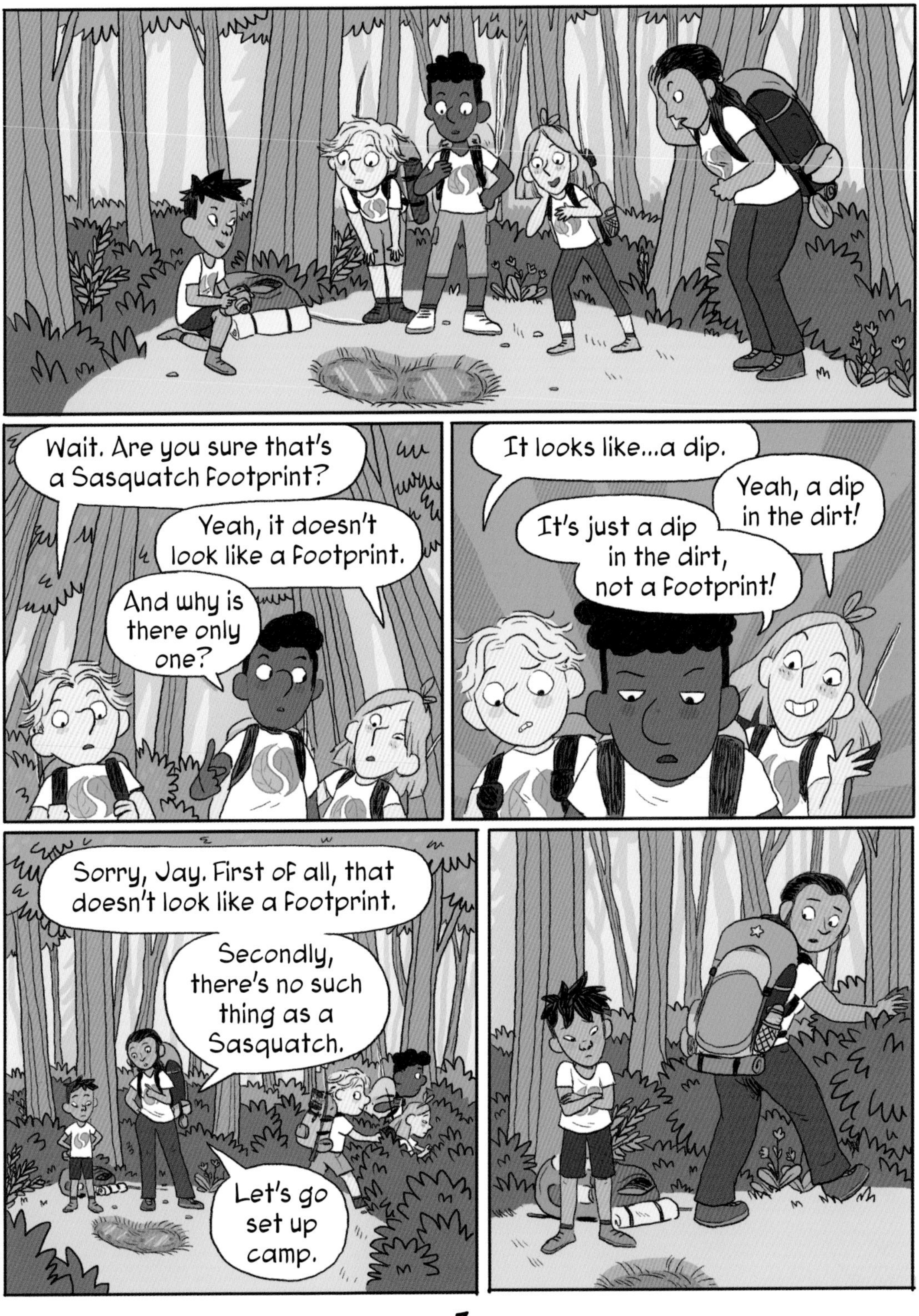

Wait. Are you sure that's a Sasquatch footprint?
Yeah, it doesn't look like a footprint.
And why is there only one?
It looks like...a dip.
It's just a dip in the dirt, not a footprint!
Yeah, a dip in the dirt!
Sorry, Jay. First of all, that doesn't look like a footprint.
Secondly, there's no such thing as a Sasquatch.
Let's go set up camp.

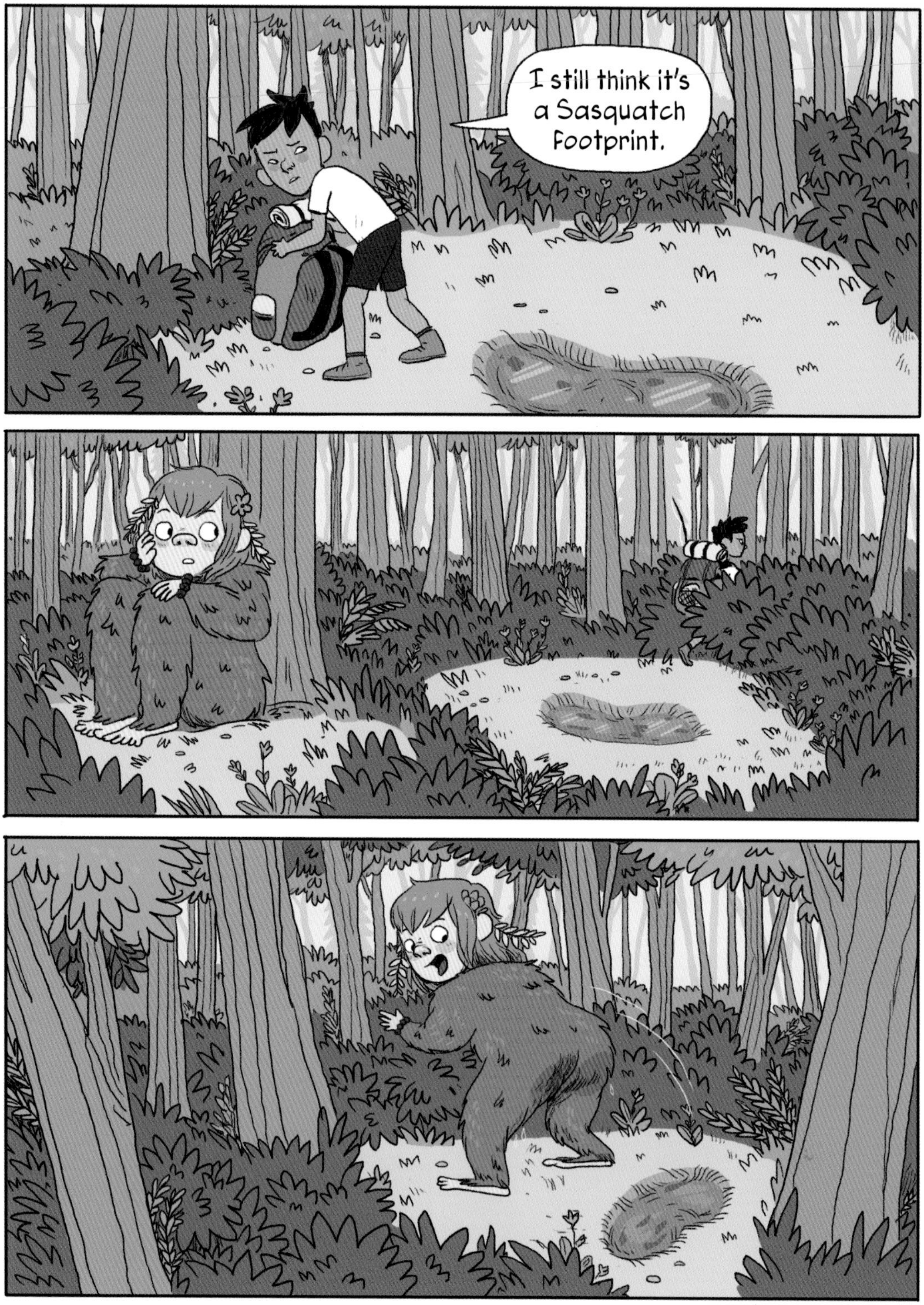
I still think it's a Sasquatch footprint.

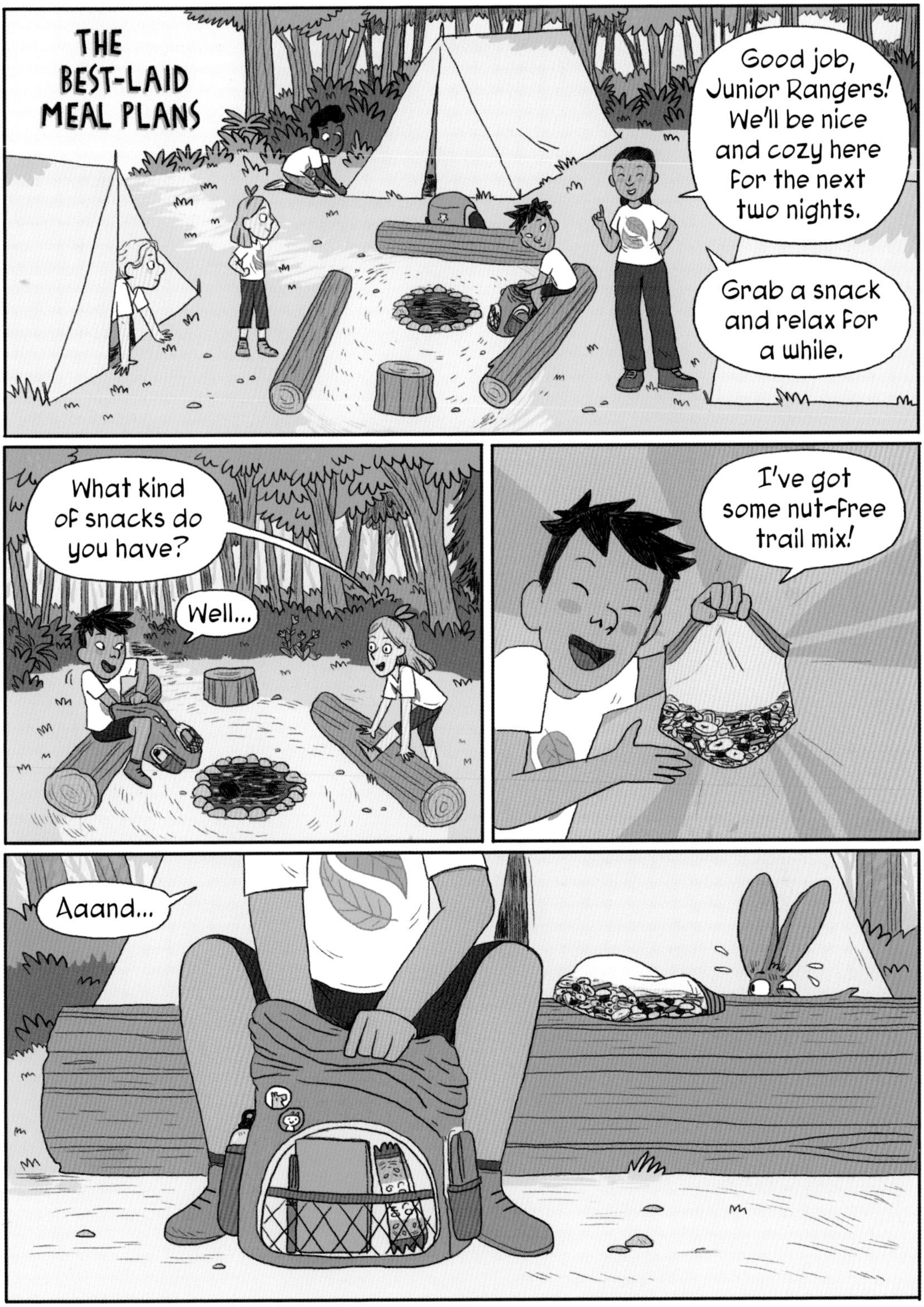
THE BEST-LAID MEAL PLANS
Good job, Junior Rangers! We'll be nice and cozy here for the next two nights.
Grab a snack and relax for a while.
What kind of snacks do you have?
Well...
I've got some nut-free trail mix!
Aaand...

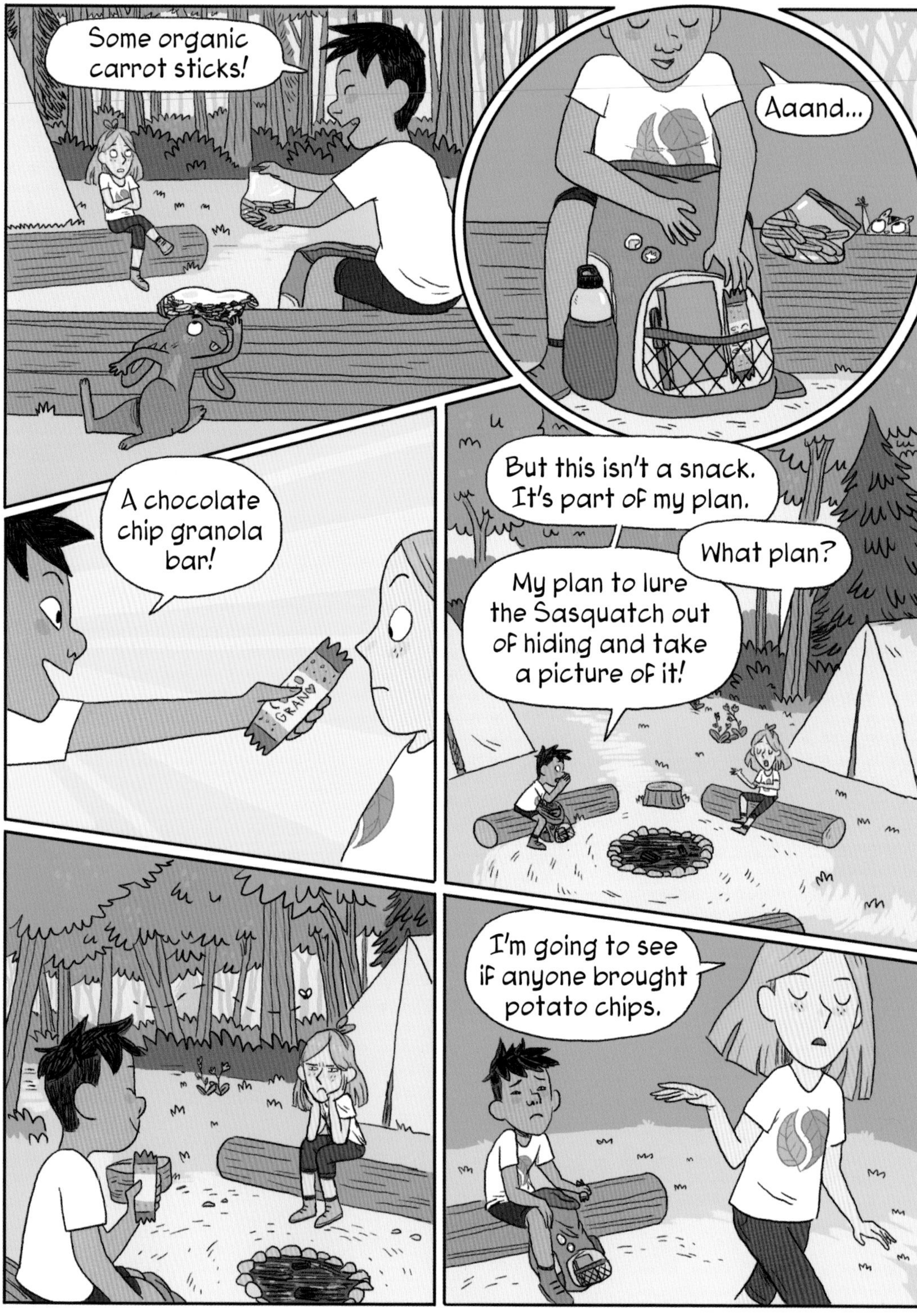
Some organic carrot sticks!
Aaand...
A chocolate chip granola bar!
GRAN
But this isn't a snack. It's part of my plan.
What plan?
My plan to lure the Sasquatch out of hiding and take a picture of it!
I'm going to see if anyone brought potato chips.

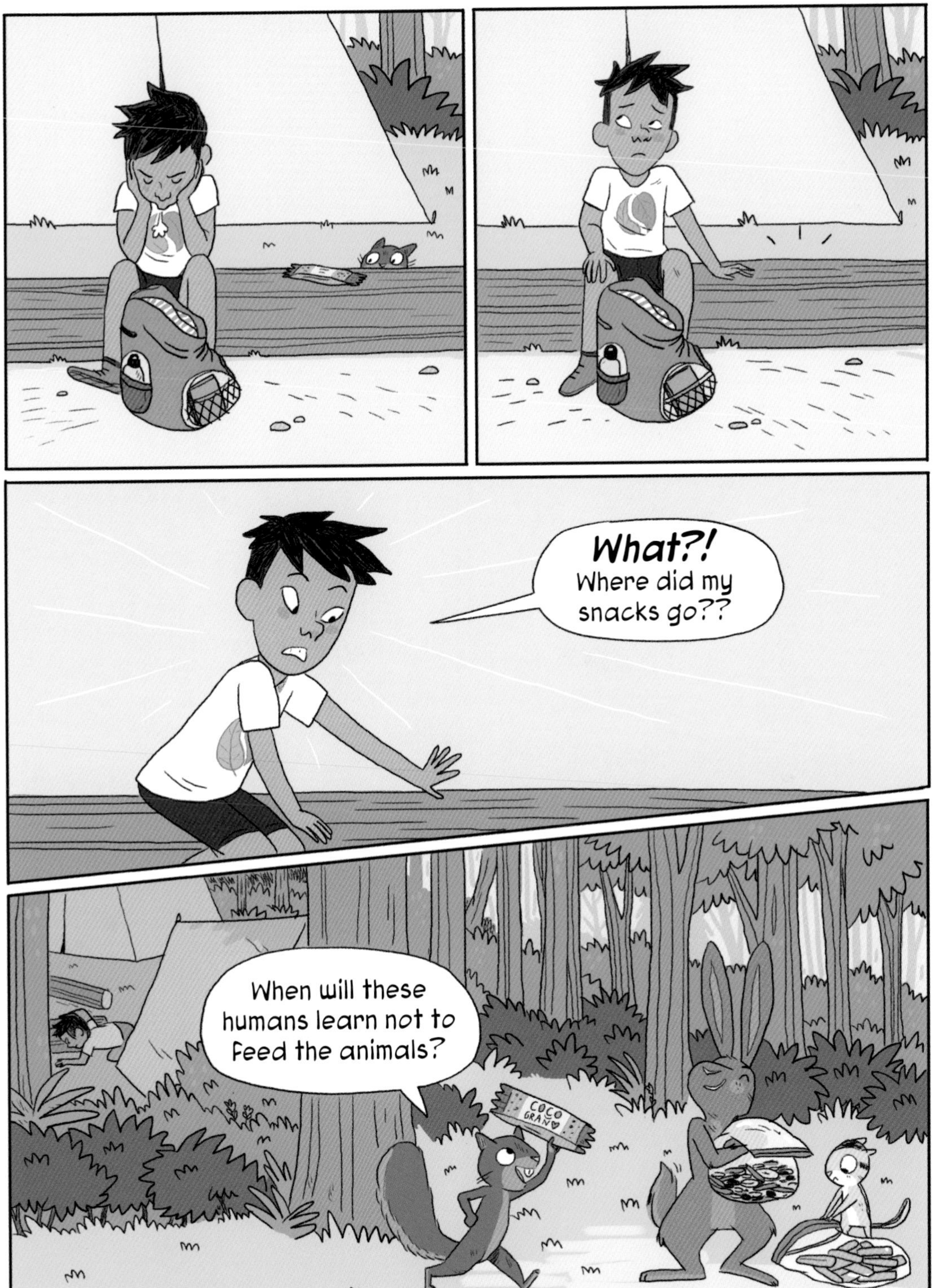
What?!
Where did my snacks go??
When will these humans learn not to feed the animals?
COCO GRAN

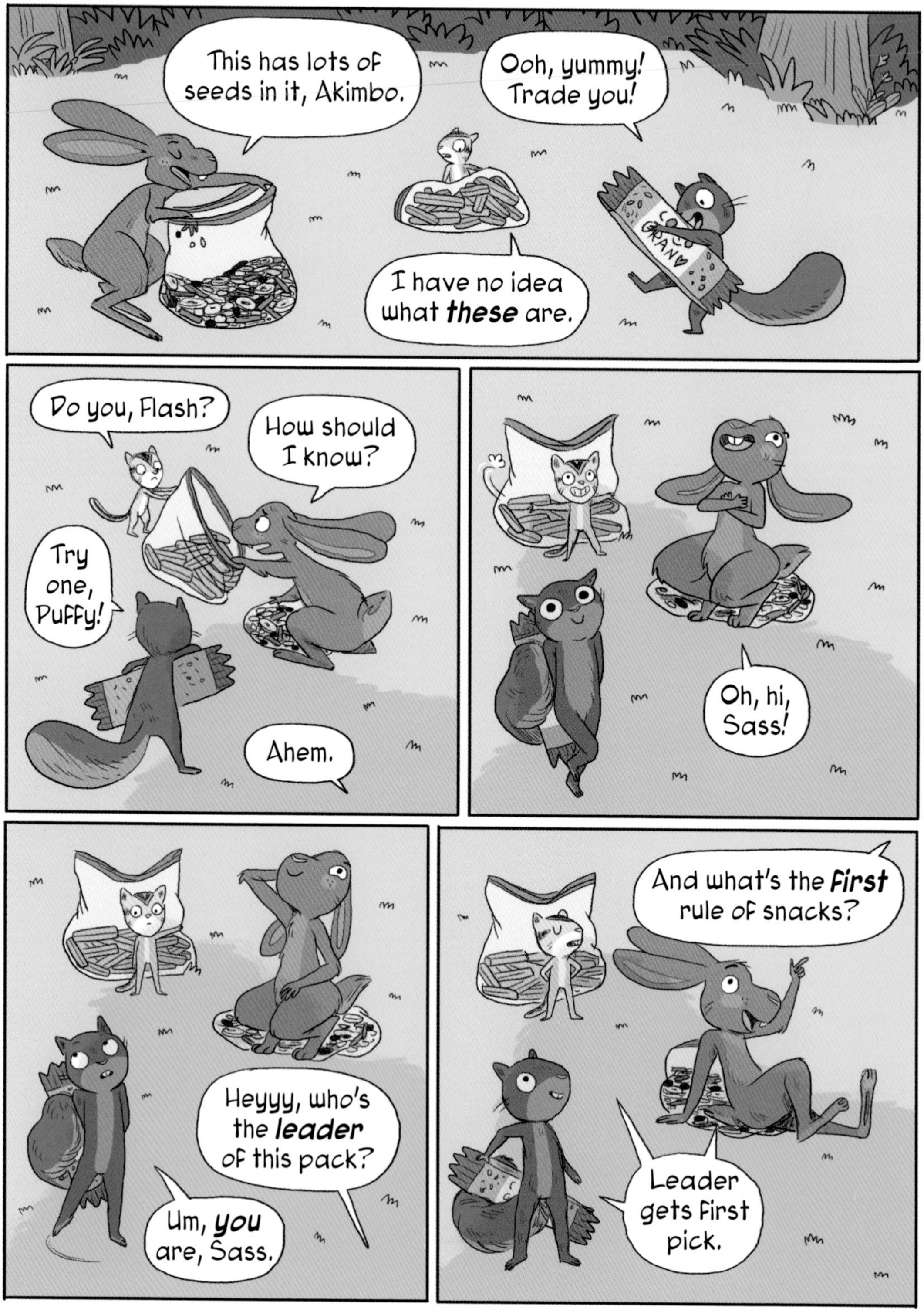

This has lots of seeds in it, Akimbo.
Ooh, yummy! Trade you!
I have no idea what **these** are.
Do you, Flash?
How should I know?
Try one, Puffy!
Ahem.
Oh, hi, Sass!
Heyyy, who's the **leader** of this pack?
Um, **you** are, Sass.
And what's the **first** rule of snacks?
Leader gets first pick.

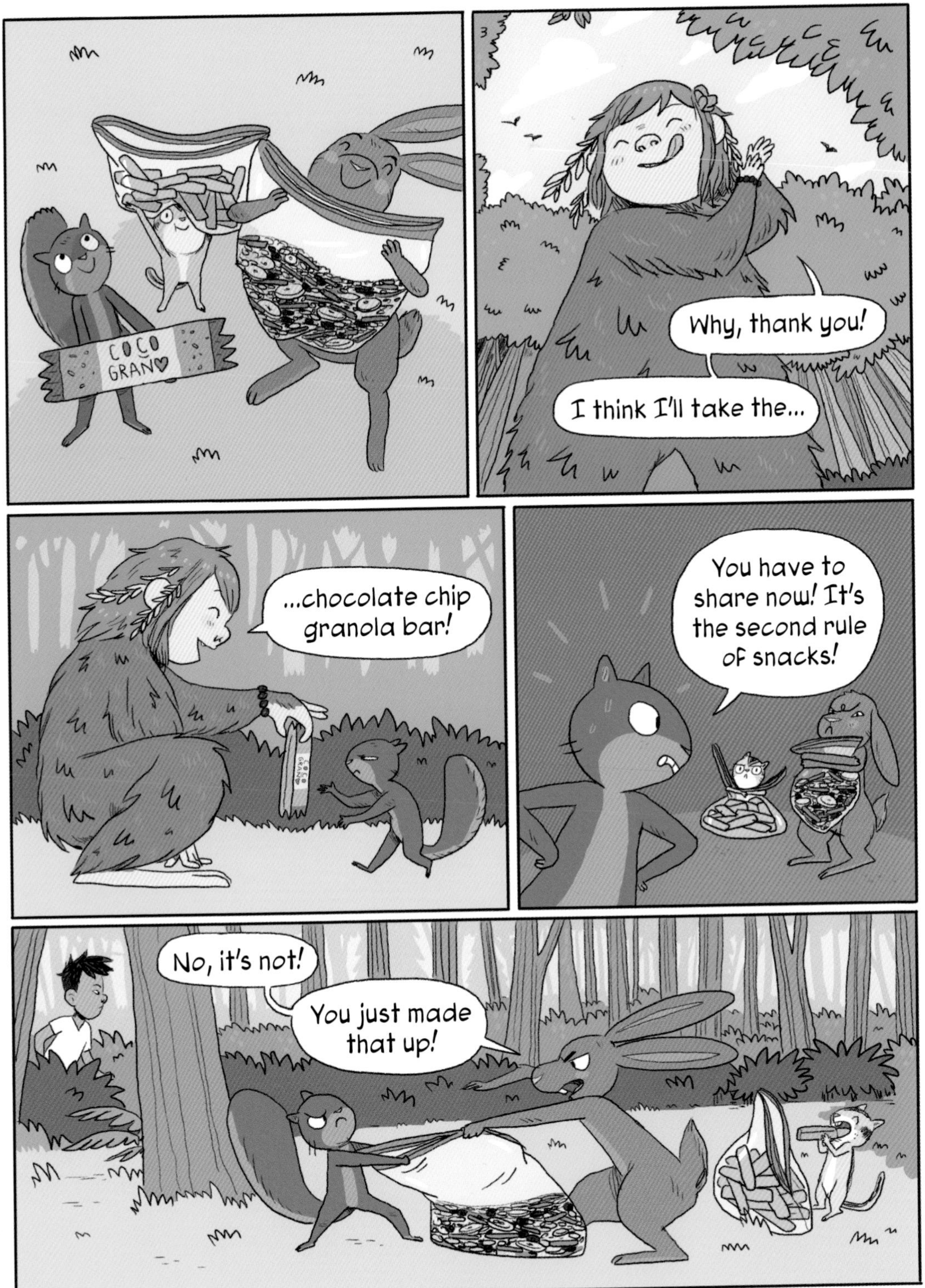
COCO GRANO
Why, thank you!
I think I'll take the...
...chocolate chip granola bar!
You have to share now! It's the second rule of snacks!
No, it's not!
You just made that up!

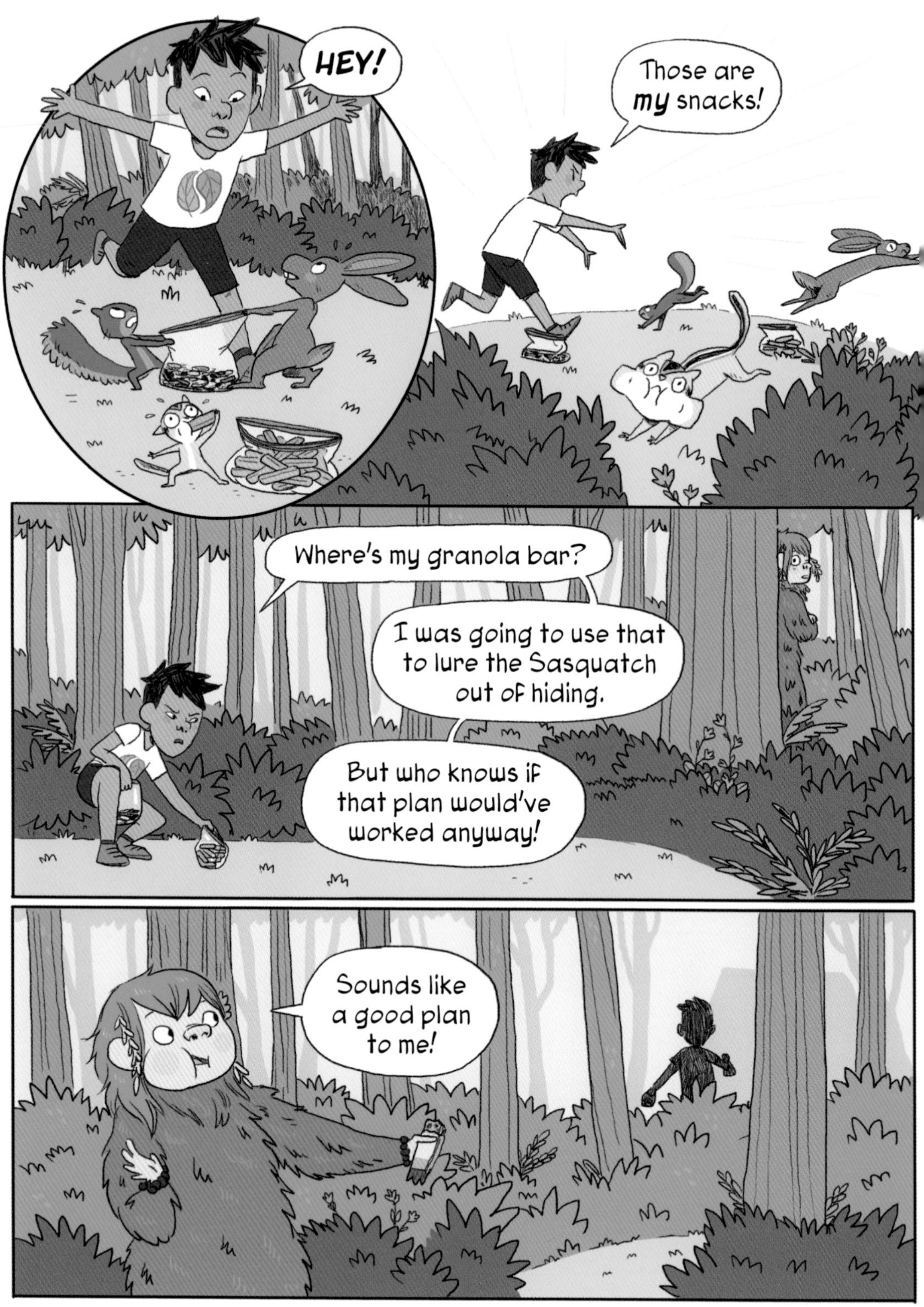
HEY!
Those are my snacks!
Where's my granola bar?
I was going to use that to lure the Sasquatch out of hiding.
But who knows if that plan would've worked anyway!
Sounds like a good plan to me!

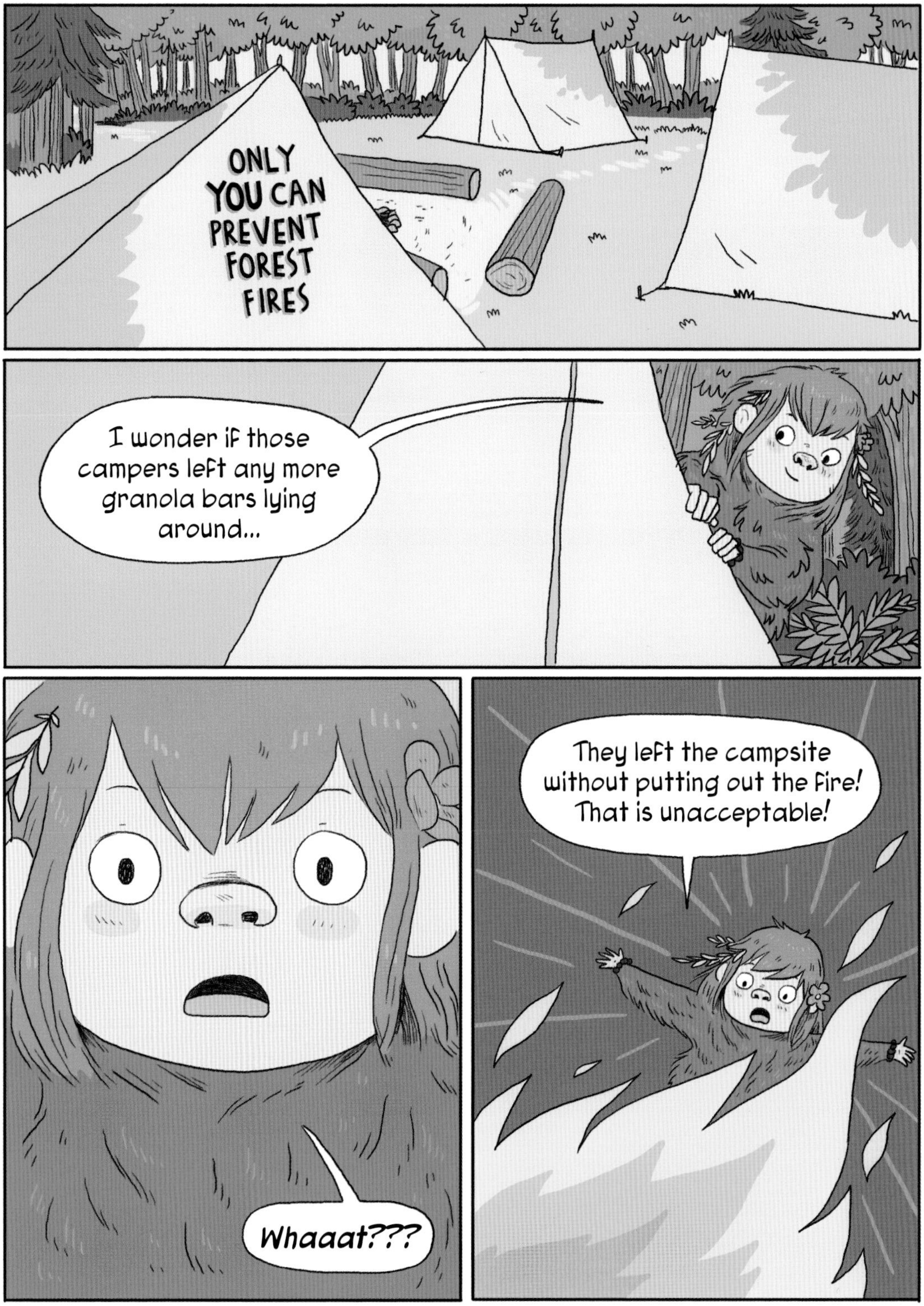
ONLY YOU CAN PREVENT FOREST FIRES
I wonder if those campers left any more granola bars lying around...
Whaaat???
They left the campsite without putting out the fire! That is unacceptable!

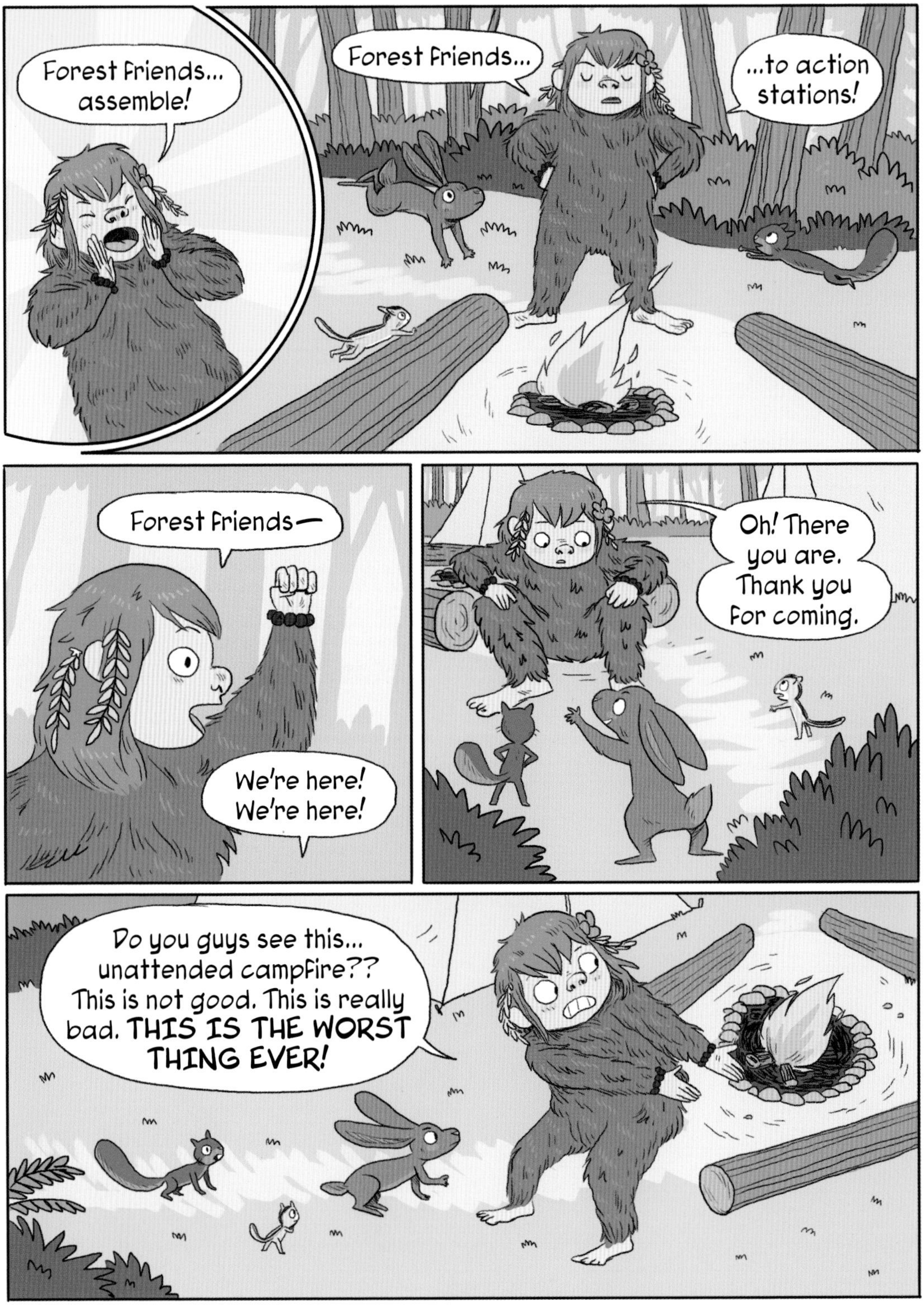
Forest friends...
assemble!
Forest friends...
...to action
stations!
Forest friends—
We're here!
We're here!
Oh! There
you are.
Thank you
for coming.
Do you guys see this...
unattended campfire??
This is not good. This is really
bad. THIS IS THE WORST
THING EVER!

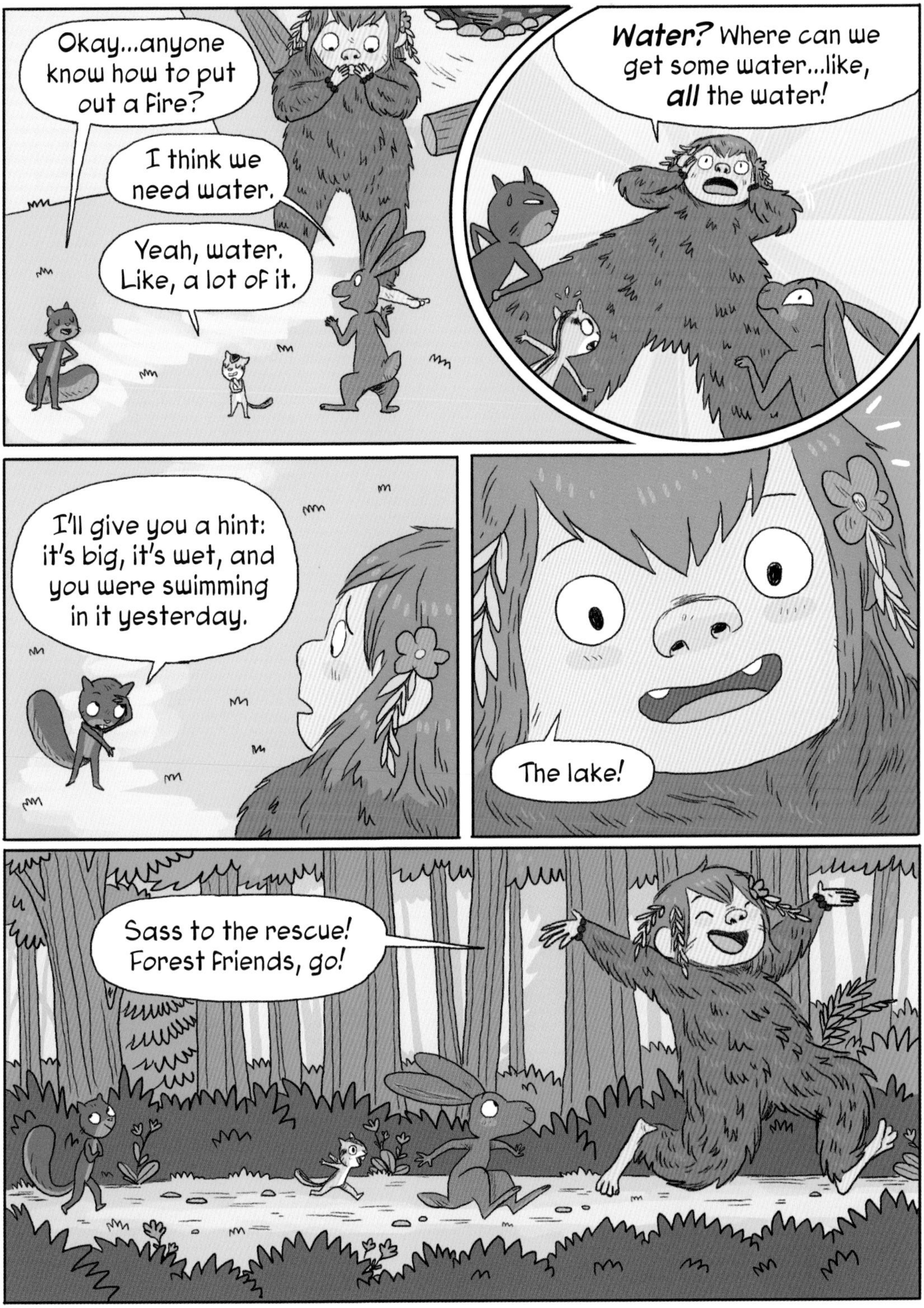

Okay...anyone know how to put out a fire?
I think we need water.
Yeah, water. Like, a lot of it.
Water? Where can we get some water...like, ***all*** the water!
I'll give you a hint: it's big, it's wet, and you were swimming in it yesterday.
The lake!
Sass to the rescue! Forest friends, go!

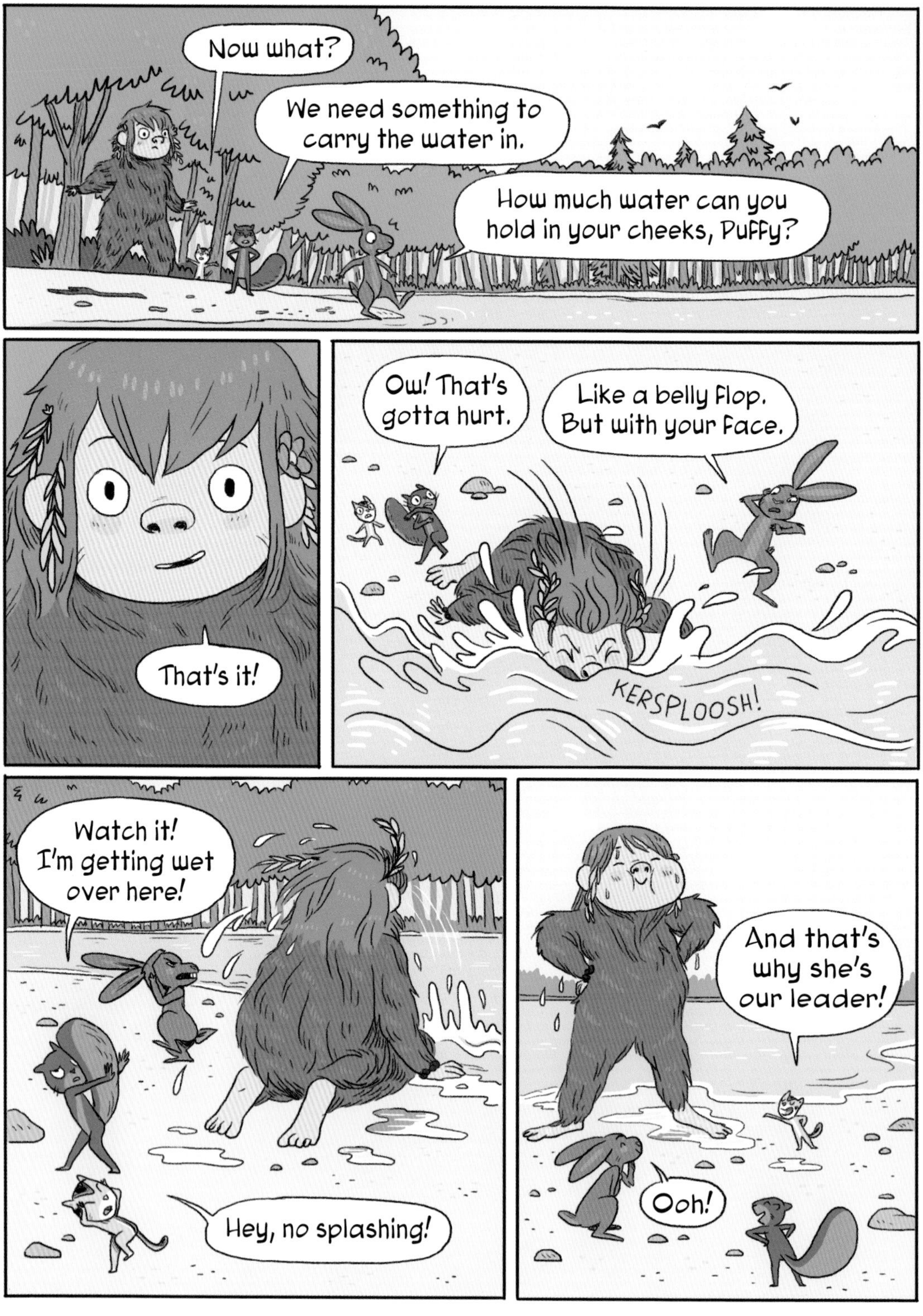
Now what?
We need something to carry the water in.
How much water can you hold in your cheeks, Puffy?
That's it!
Ow! That's gotta hurt.
Like a belly flop. But with your face.
KERSPLOOSH!
Watch it! I'm getting wet over here!
Hey, no splashing!
And that's why she's our leader!
Ooh!

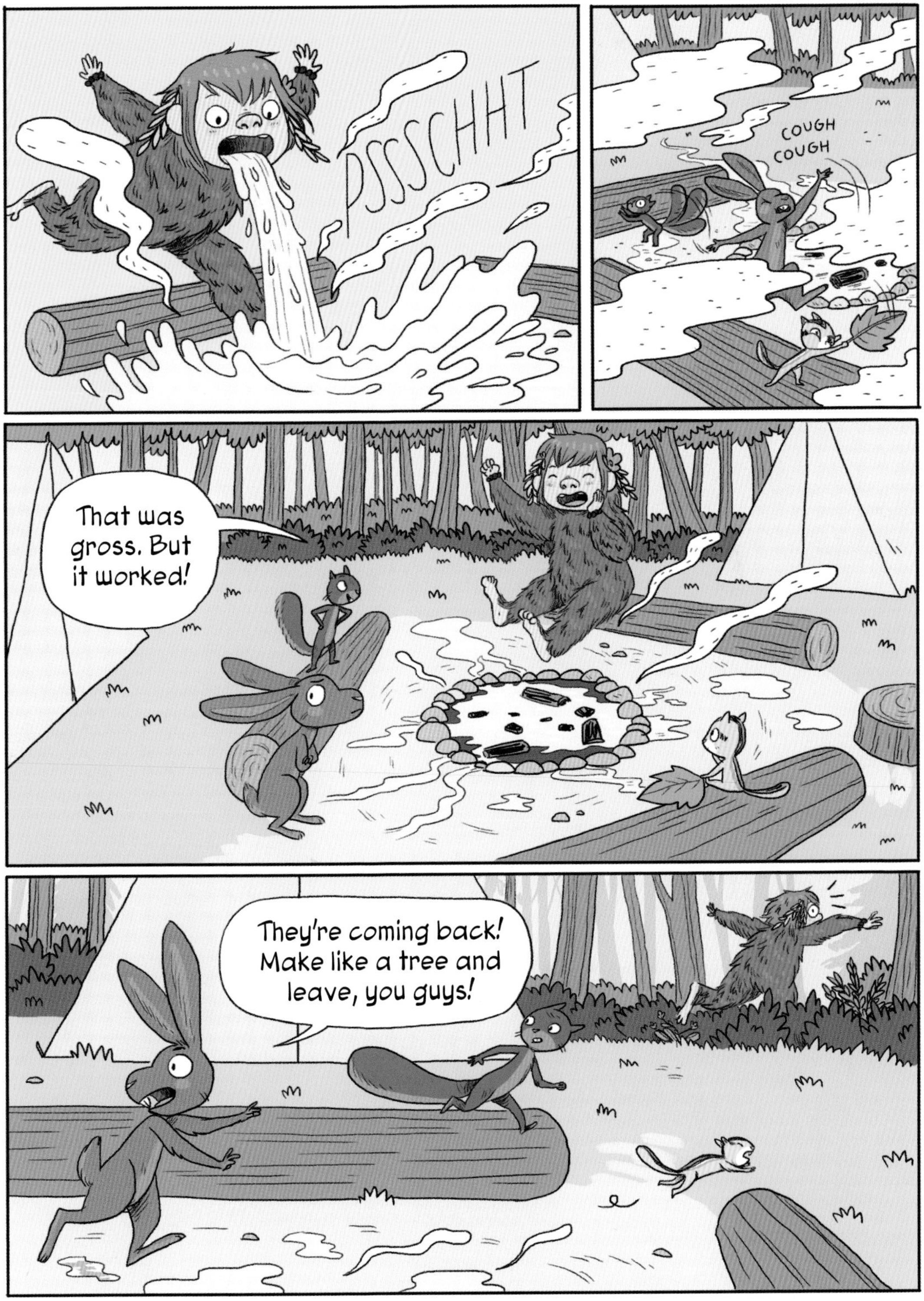
PSSSCHHT
COUGH COUGH
That was gross. But it worked!
They're coming back! Make like a tree and leave, you guys!

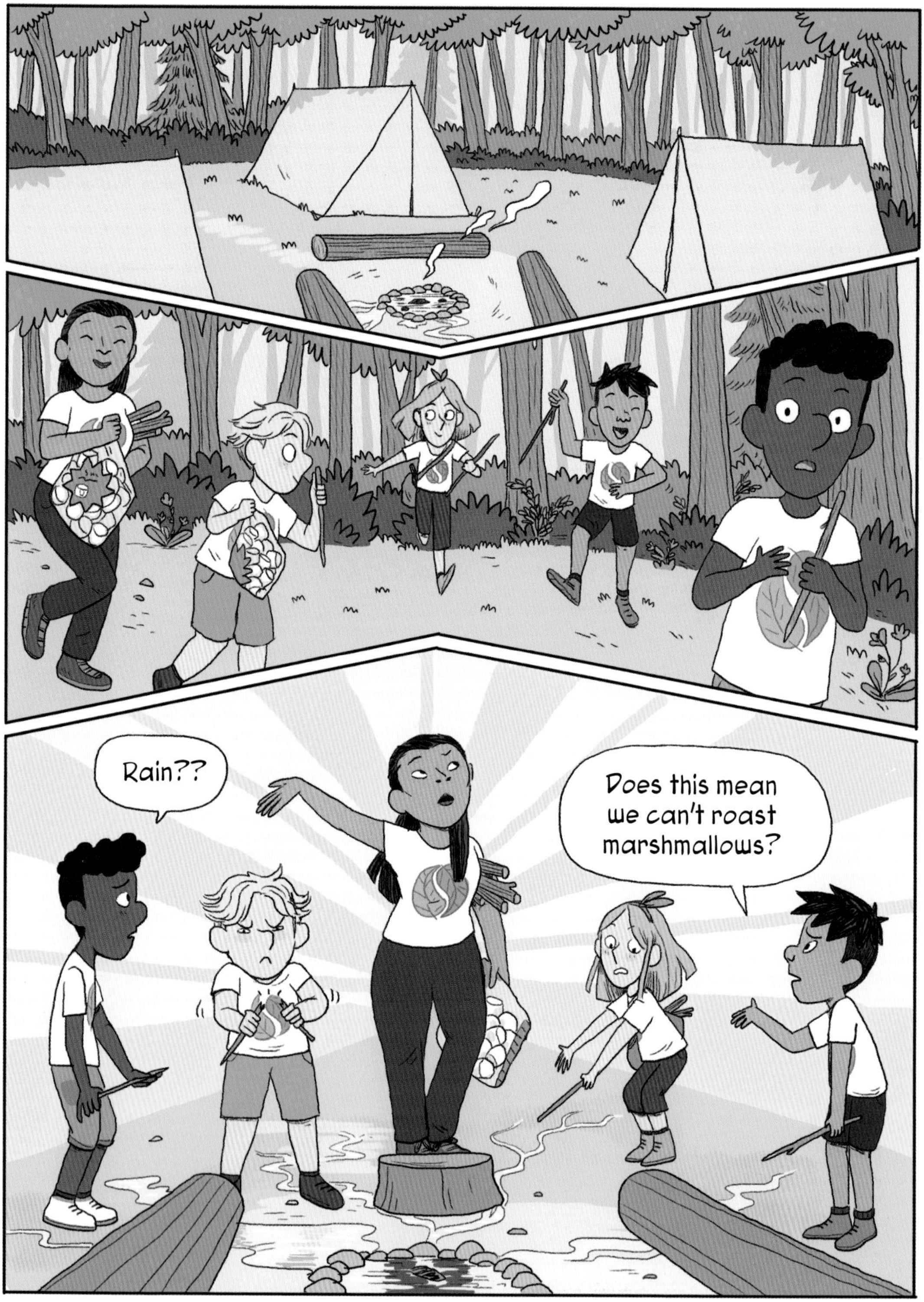
Rain??
Does this mean we can't roast marshmallows?

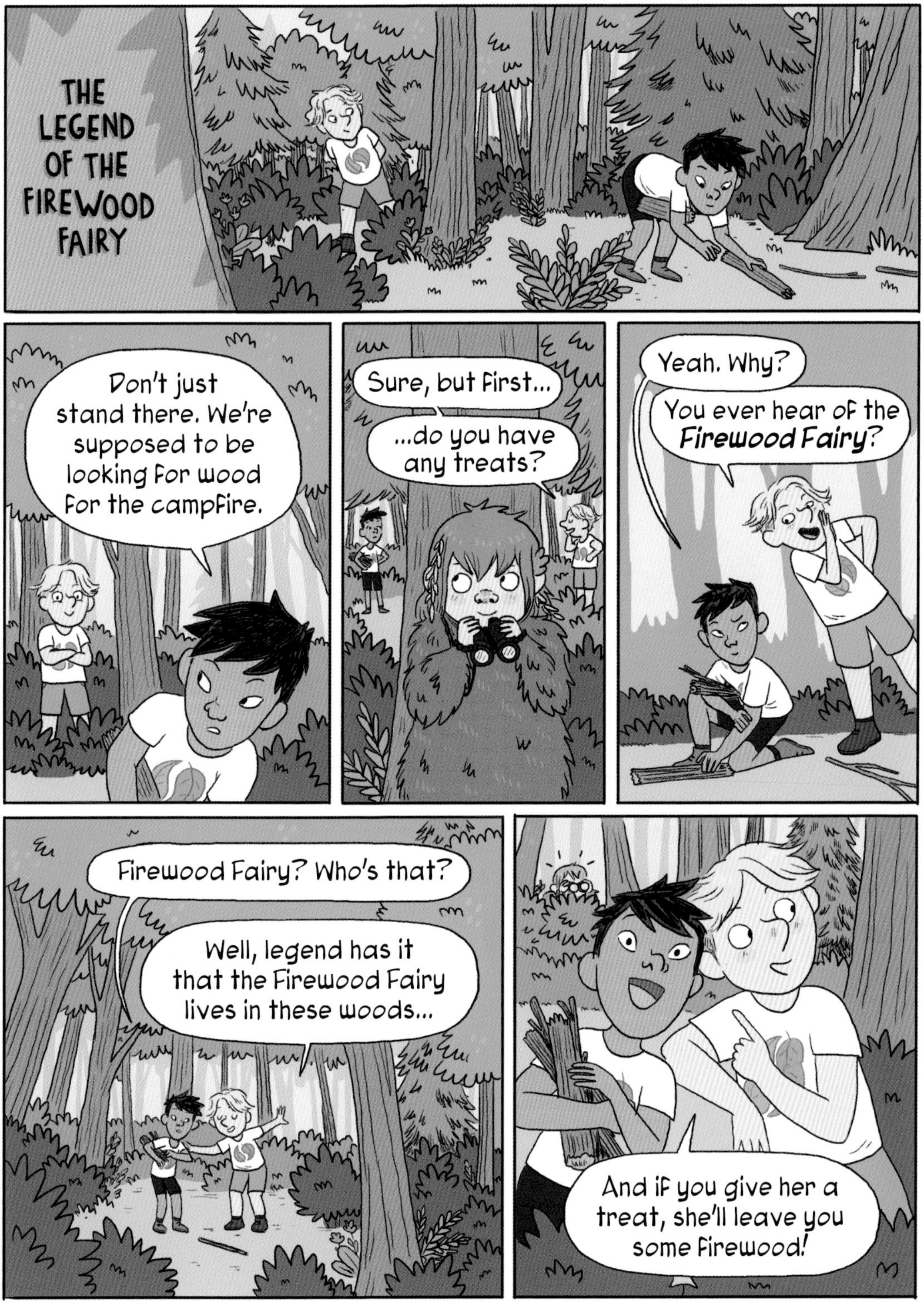
THE LEGEND OF THE FIREWOOD FAIRY
Don't just stand there. We're supposed to be looking for wood for the campfire.
Sure, but first...
...do you have any treats?
Yeah. Why?
You ever hear of the *Firewood Fairy*?
Firewood Fairy? Who's that?
Well, legend has it that the Firewood Fairy lives in these woods...
And if you give her a treat, she'll leave you some firewood!

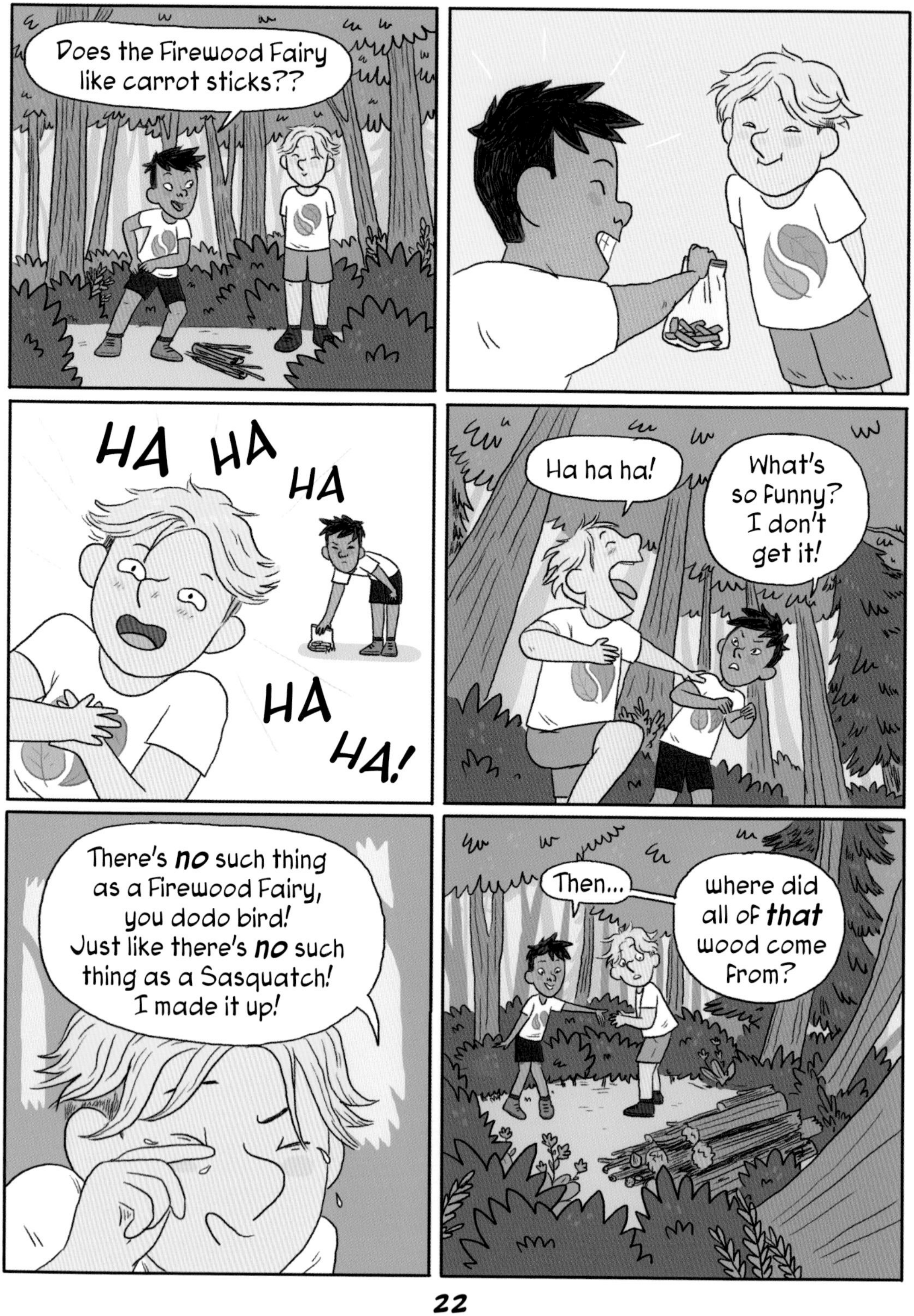
Does the Firewood Fairy like carrot sticks??
HA HA HA
HA HA!
Ha ha ha!
What's so funny? I don't get it!
There's **no** such thing as a Firewood Fairy, you dodo bird! Just like there's **no** such thing as a Sasquatch! I made it up!
Then...
where did all of ***that*** wood come from?

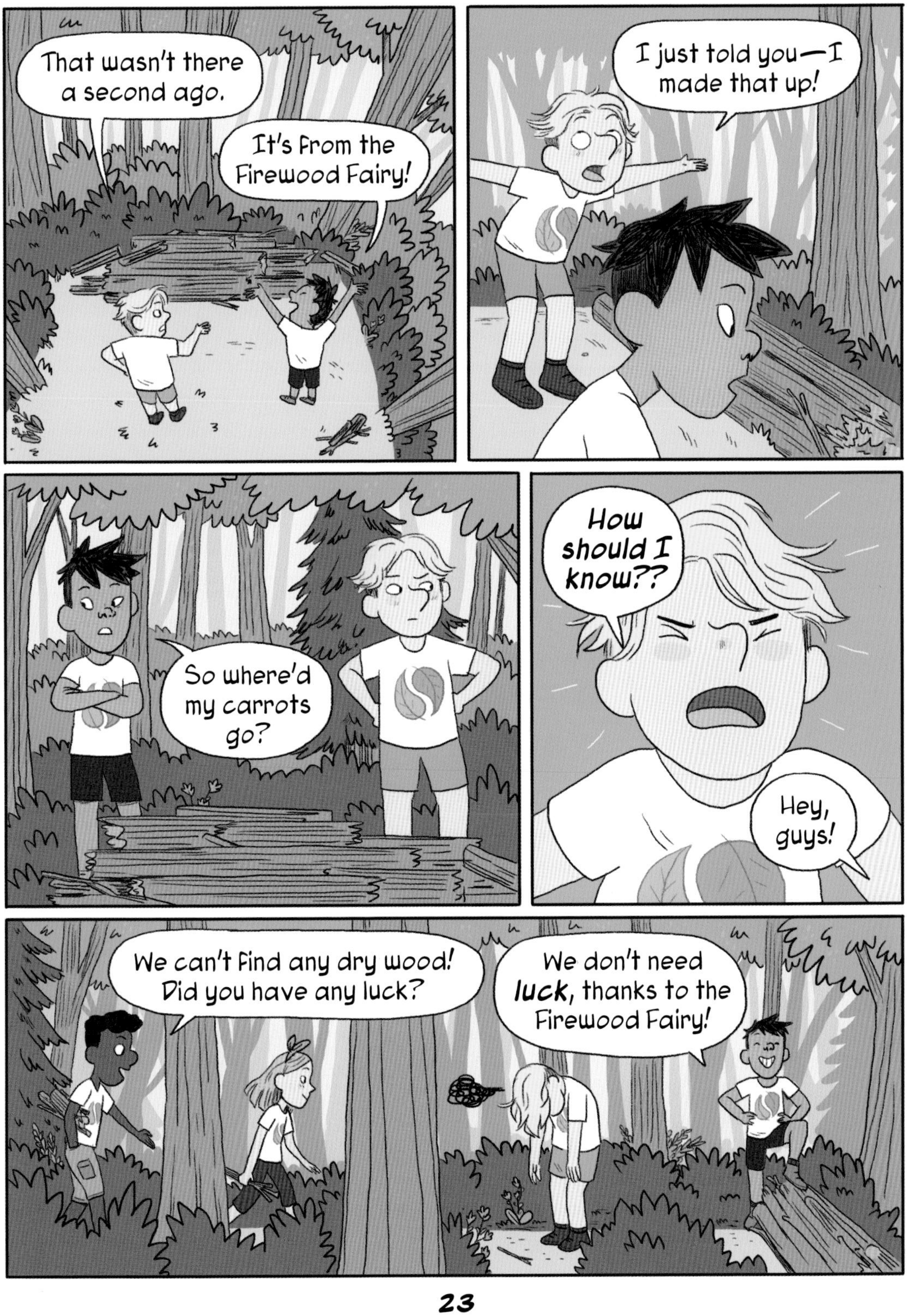
That wasn't there a second ago.
It's from the Firewood Fairy!
I just told you—I made that up!
So where'd my carrots go?
How should I know??
Hey, guys!
We can't find any dry wood! Did you have any luck?
We don't need **luck**, thanks to the Firewood Fairy!

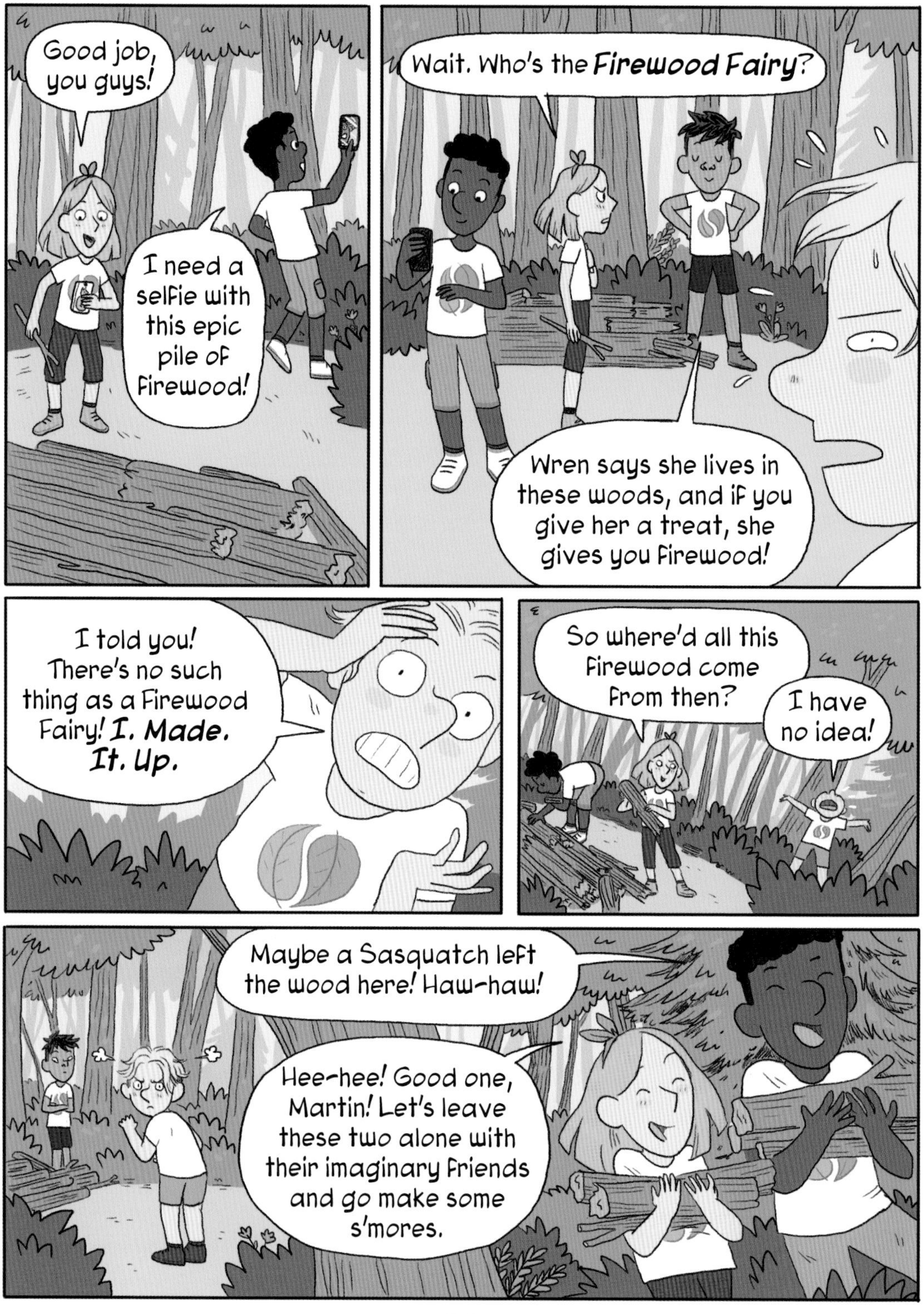
Good job, you guys!
I need a selfie with this epic pile of firewood!
Wait. Who's the **Firewood Fairy**?
Wren says she lives in these woods, and if you give her a treat, she gives you firewood!
I told you! There's no such thing as a Firewood Fairy! **I. Made. It. Up.**
So where'd all this firewood come from then?
I have no idea!
Maybe a Sasquatch left the wood here! Haw-haw!
Hee-hee! Good one, Martin! Let's leave these two alone with their imaginary friends and go make some s'mores.

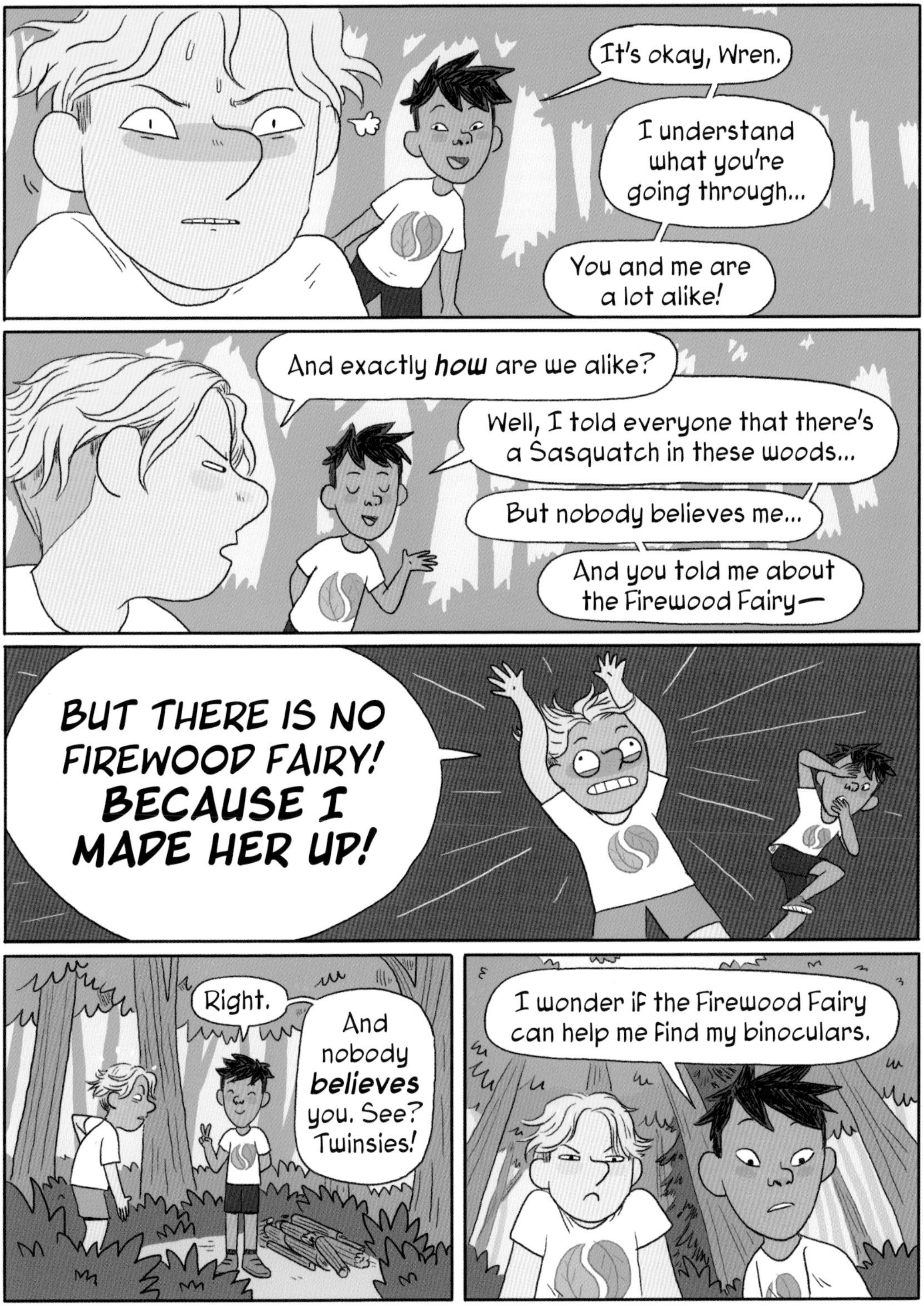
It's okay, Wren.
I understand what you're going through...
You and me are a lot alike!
And exactly **how** are we alike?
Well, I told everyone that there's a Sasquatch in these woods...
But nobody believes me...
And you told me about the Firewood Fairy—
BUT THERE IS NO FIREWOOD FAIRY! BECAUSE I MADE HER UP!
Right.
And nobody **believes** you. See? Twinsies!
I wonder if the Firewood Fairy can help me find my binoculars.

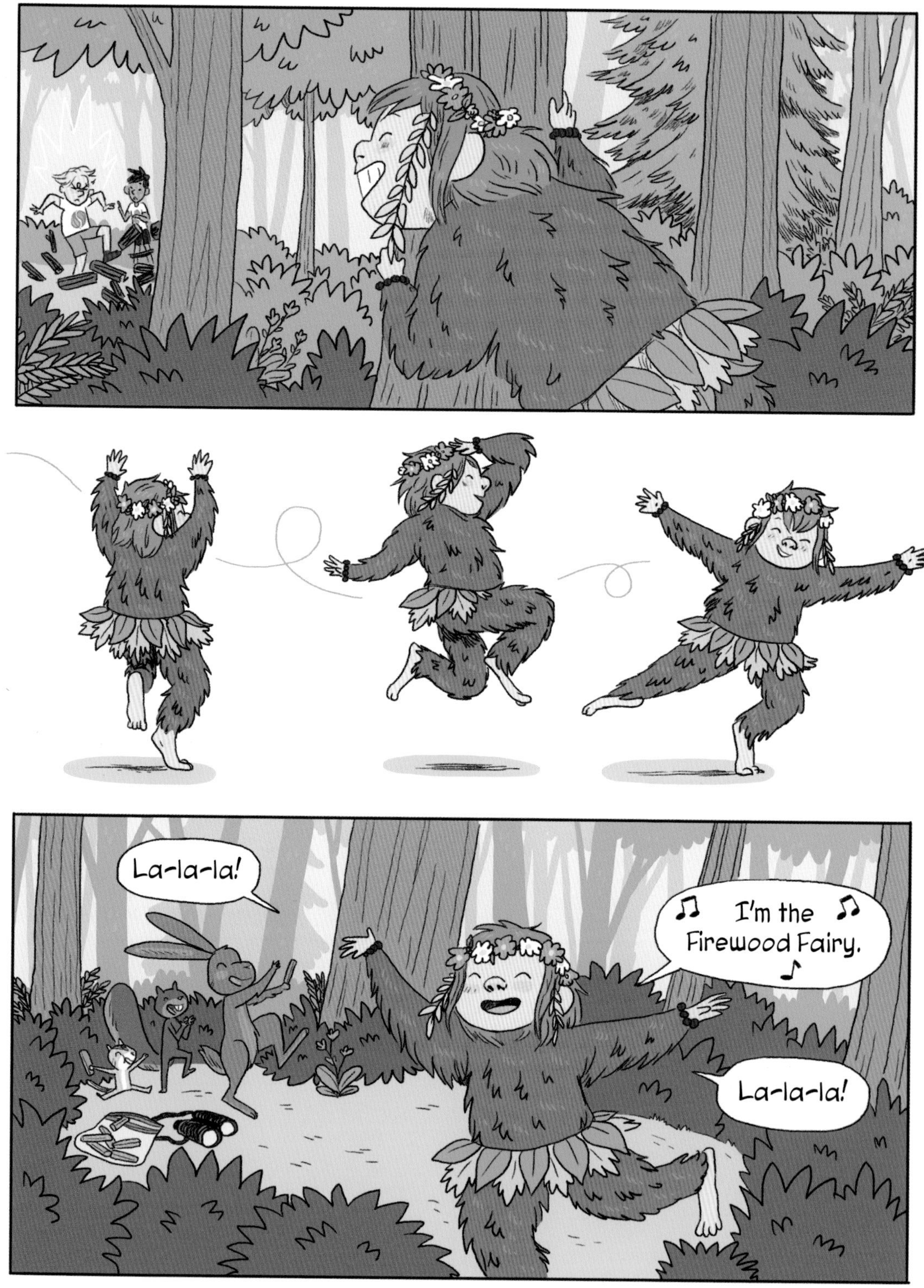
La-la-la!
♫ I'm the ♫ Firewood Fairy. ♪
La-la-la!

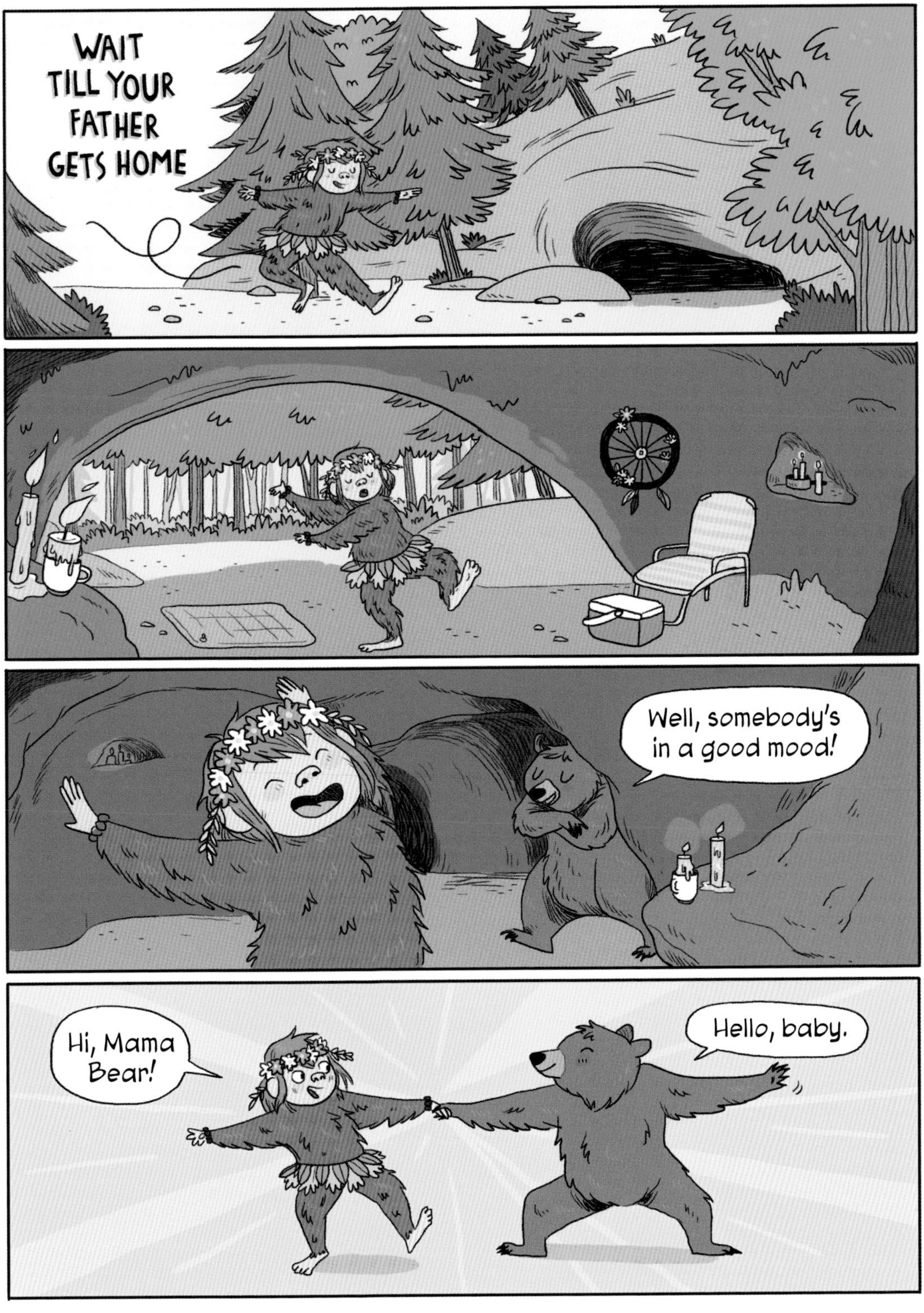
WAIT TILL YOUR FATHER GETS HOME
Well, somebody's in a good mood!
Hi, Mama Bear!
Hello, baby.

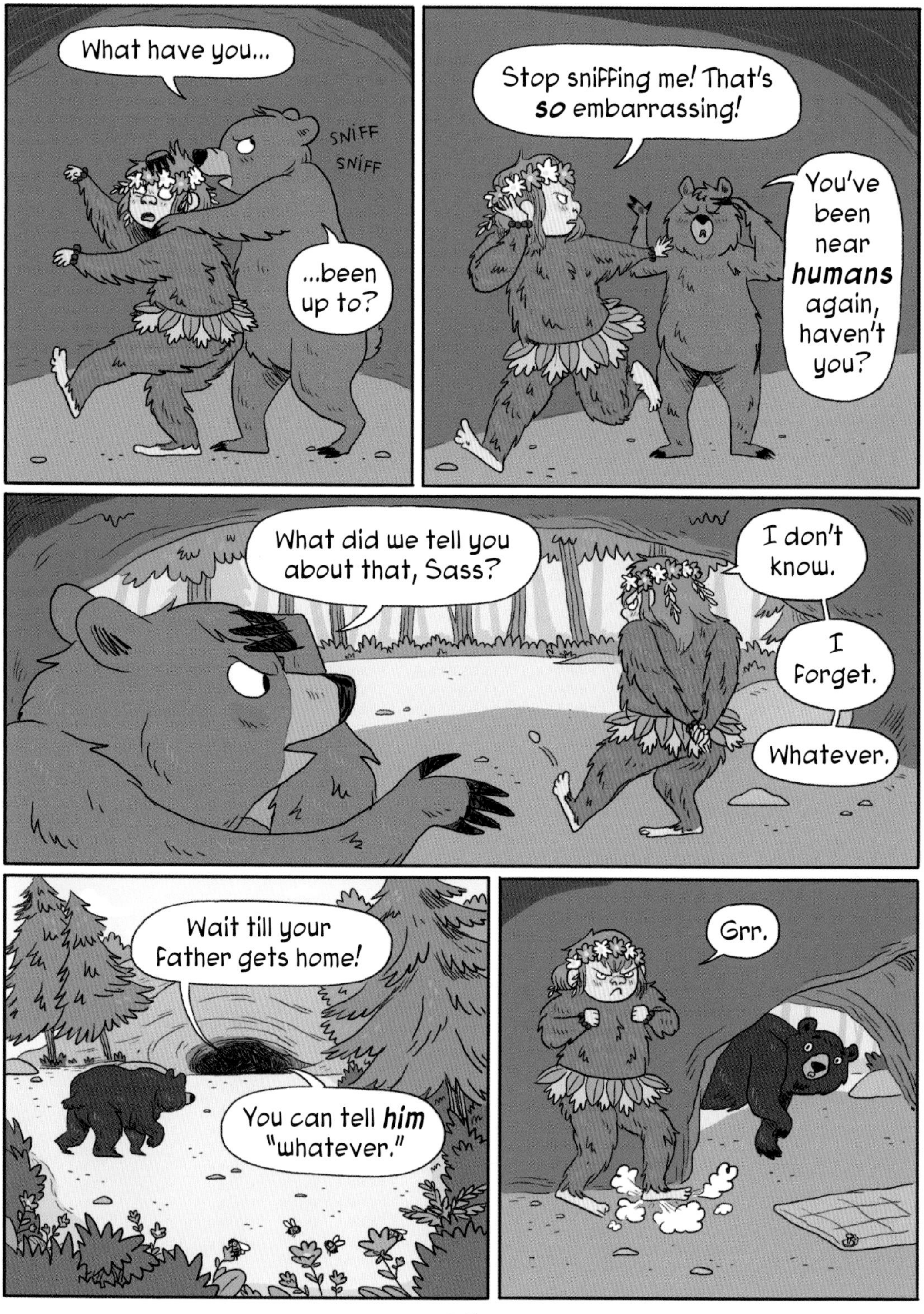
What have you...
SNIFF
SNIFF
...been up to?
Stop sniffing me! That's **so** embarrassing!
You've been near **humans** again, haven't you?
What did we tell you about that, Sass?
I don't know.
I forget.
Whatever.
Wait till your father gets home!
You can tell **him** "whatever."
Grr.

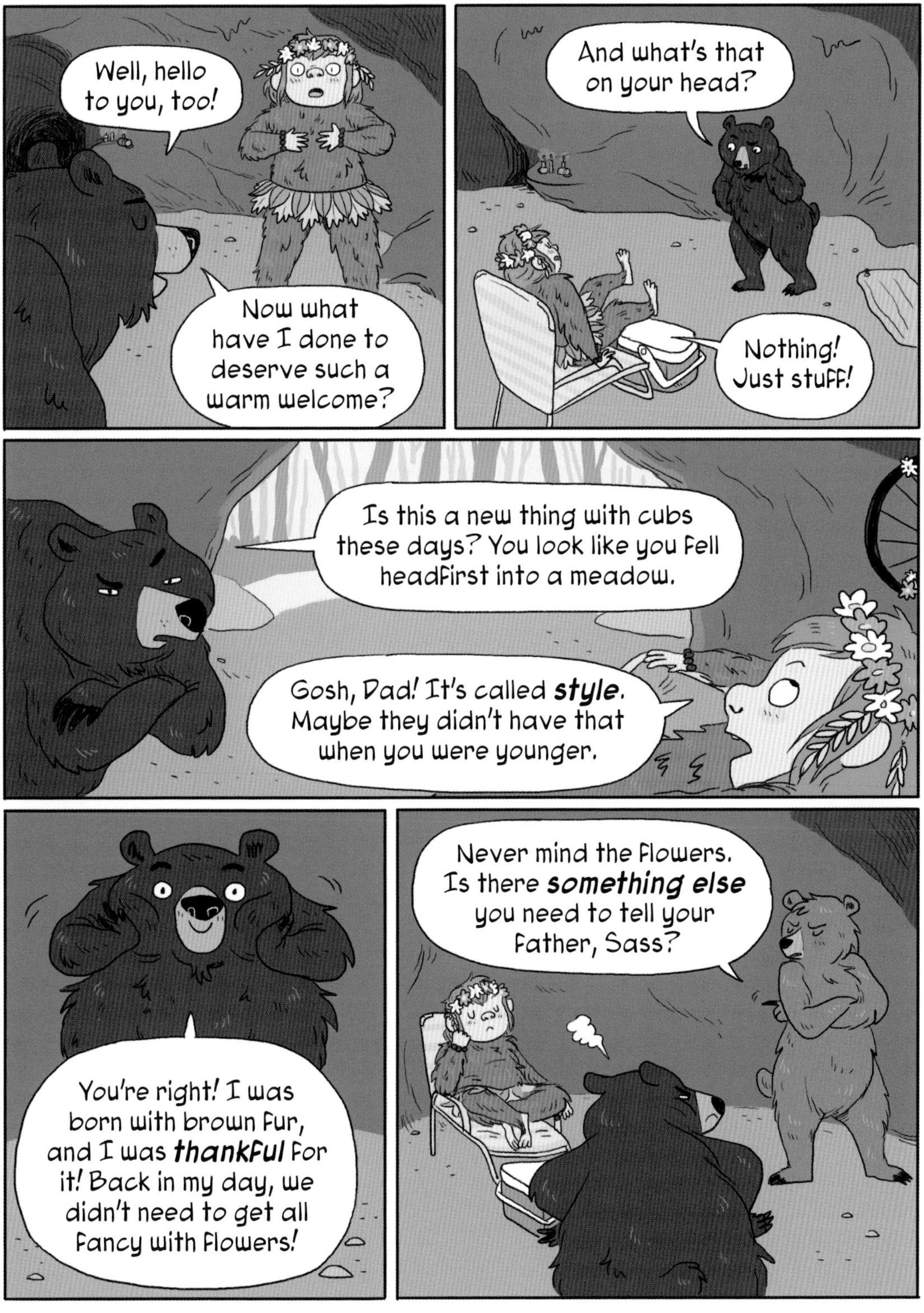
Well, hello to you, too!
Now what have I done to deserve such a warm welcome?
And what's that on your head?
Nothing! Just stuff!
Is this a new thing with cubs these days? You look like you fell headfirst into a meadow.
Gosh, Dad! It's called **style**. Maybe they didn't have that when you were younger.
You're right! I was born with brown fur, and I was **thankful** for it! Back in my day, we didn't need to get all fancy with flowers!
Never mind the flowers. Is there **something else** you need to tell your father, Sass?

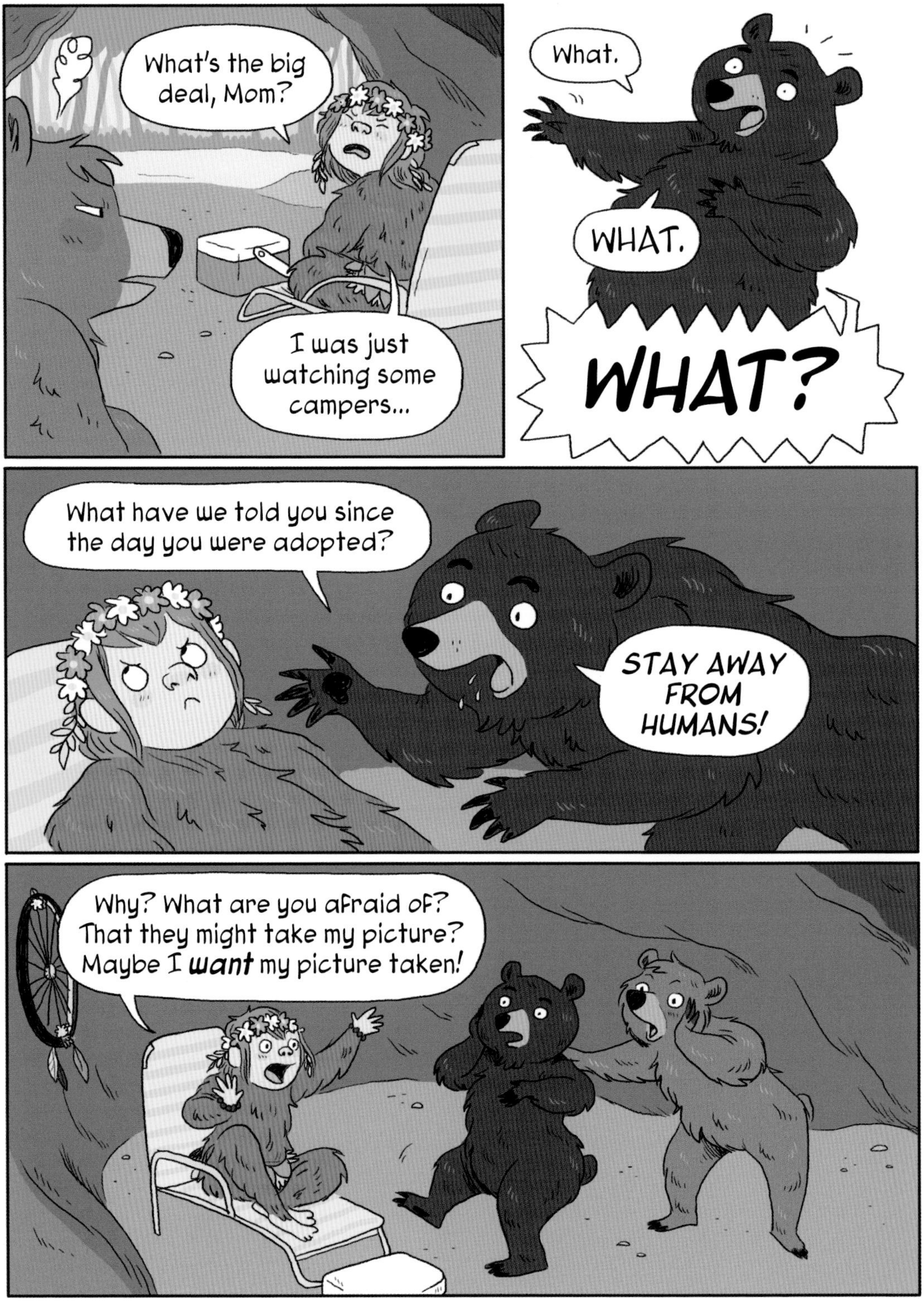
What's the big deal, Mom?
I was just watching some campers...
What.
WHAT.
WHAT?
What have we told you since the day you were adopted?
STAY AWAY FROM HUMANS!
Why? What are you afraid of? That they might take my picture? Maybe I *want* my picture taken!

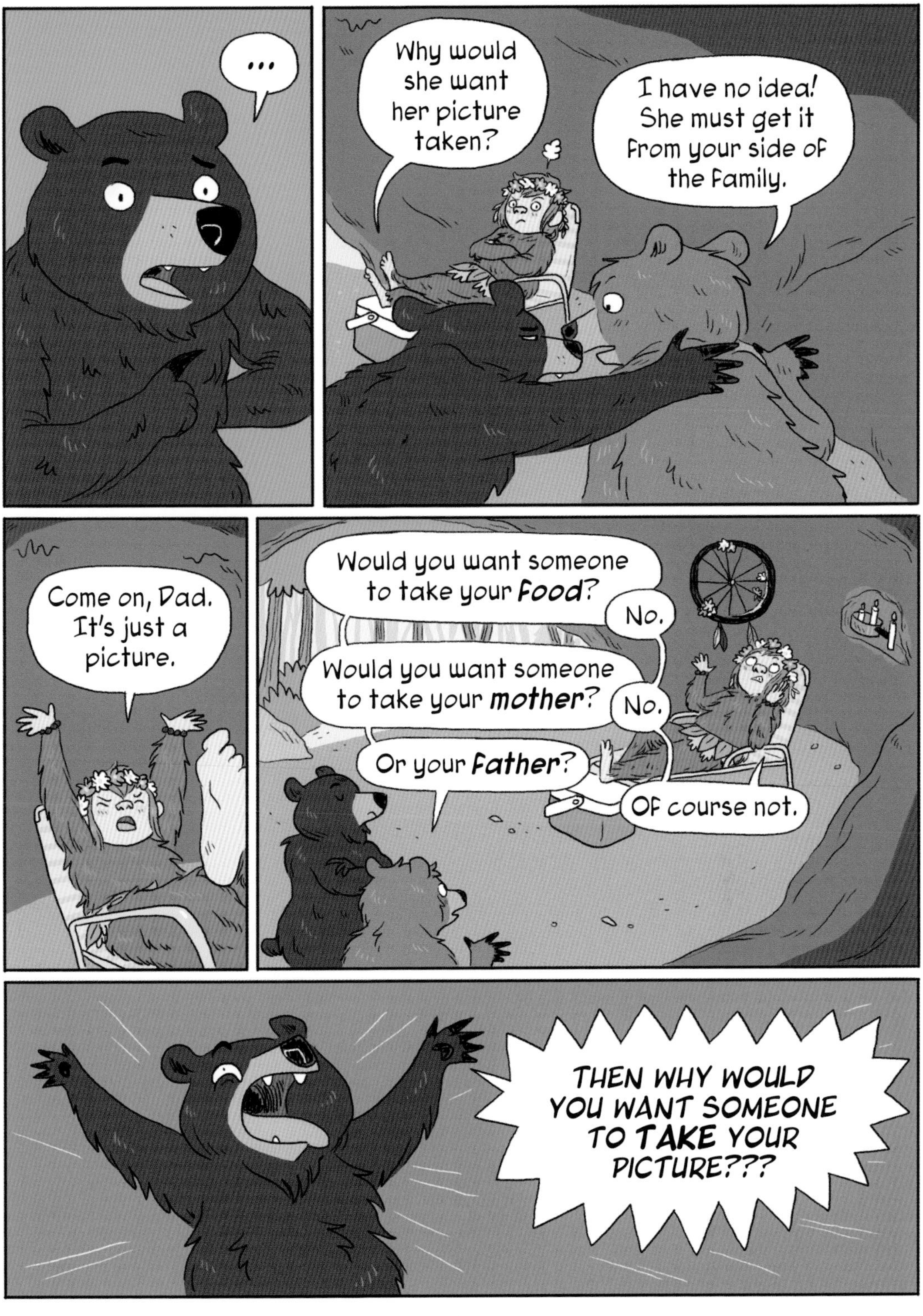
...
Why would she want her picture taken?
I have no idea! She must get it from your side of the family.
Come on, Dad. It's just a picture.
Would you want someone to take your **food**?
No.
Would you want someone to take your **mother**?
No.
Or your **father**?
Of course not.
THEN WHY WOULD YOU WANT SOMEONE TO **TAKE** YOUR PICTURE???

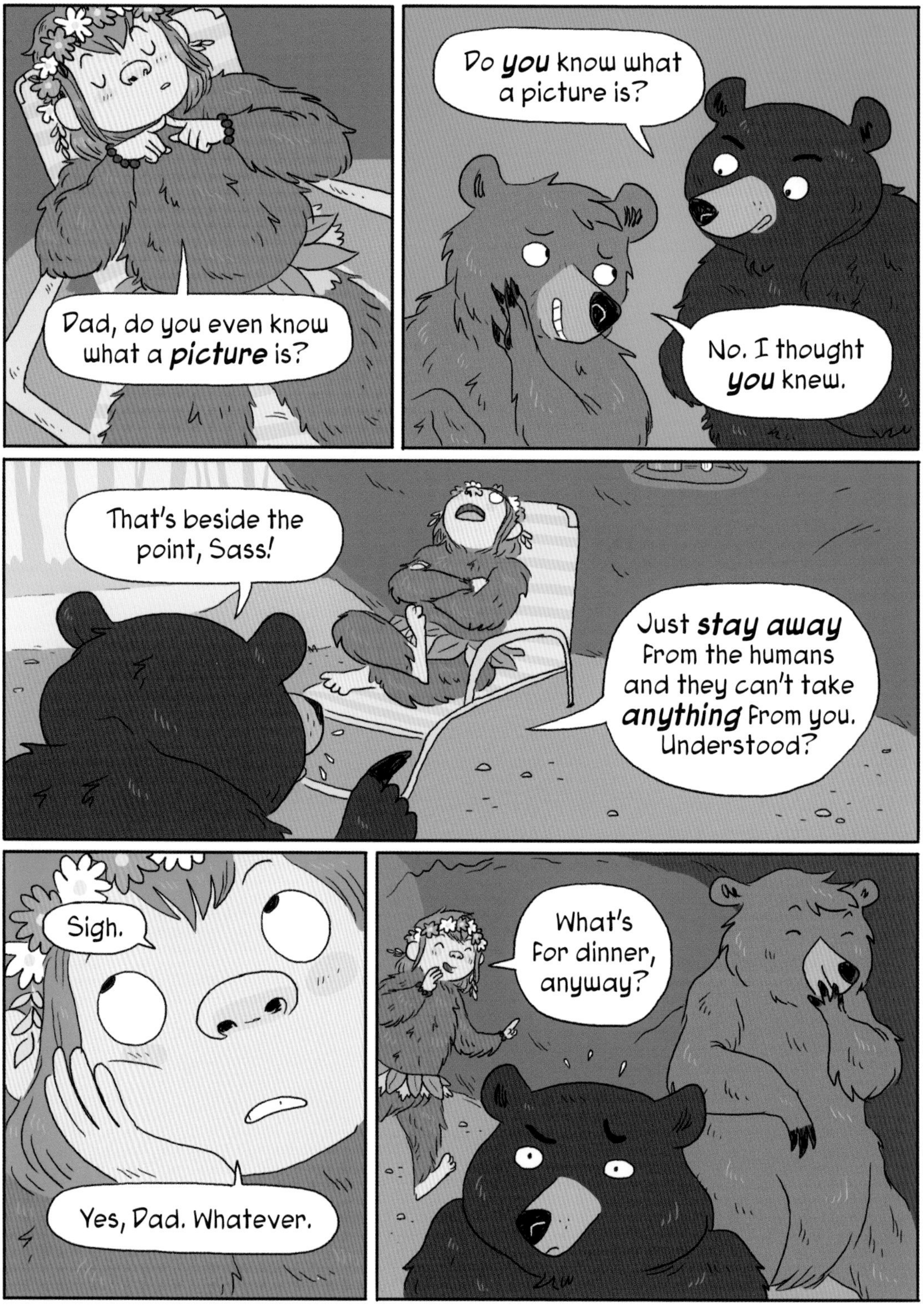

Dad, do you even know what a **picture** is?
Do **you** know what a picture is?
No. I thought **you** knew.
That's beside the point, Sass!
Just **stay away** from the humans and they can't take **anything** from you. Understood?
Sigh.
Yes, Dad. Whatever.
What's for dinner, anyway?

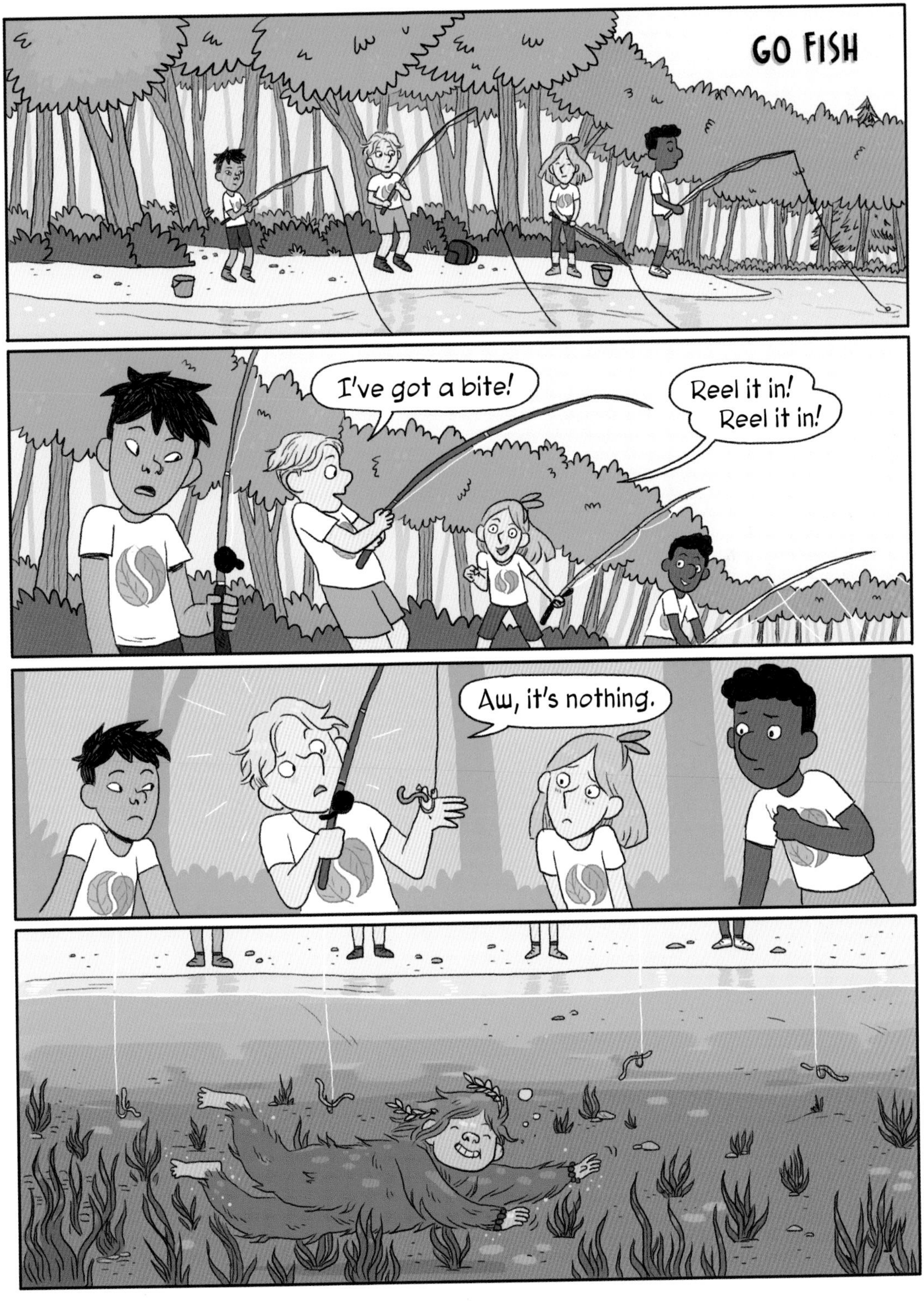
GO FISH
I've got a bite!
Reel it in! Reel it in!
Aw, it's nothing.

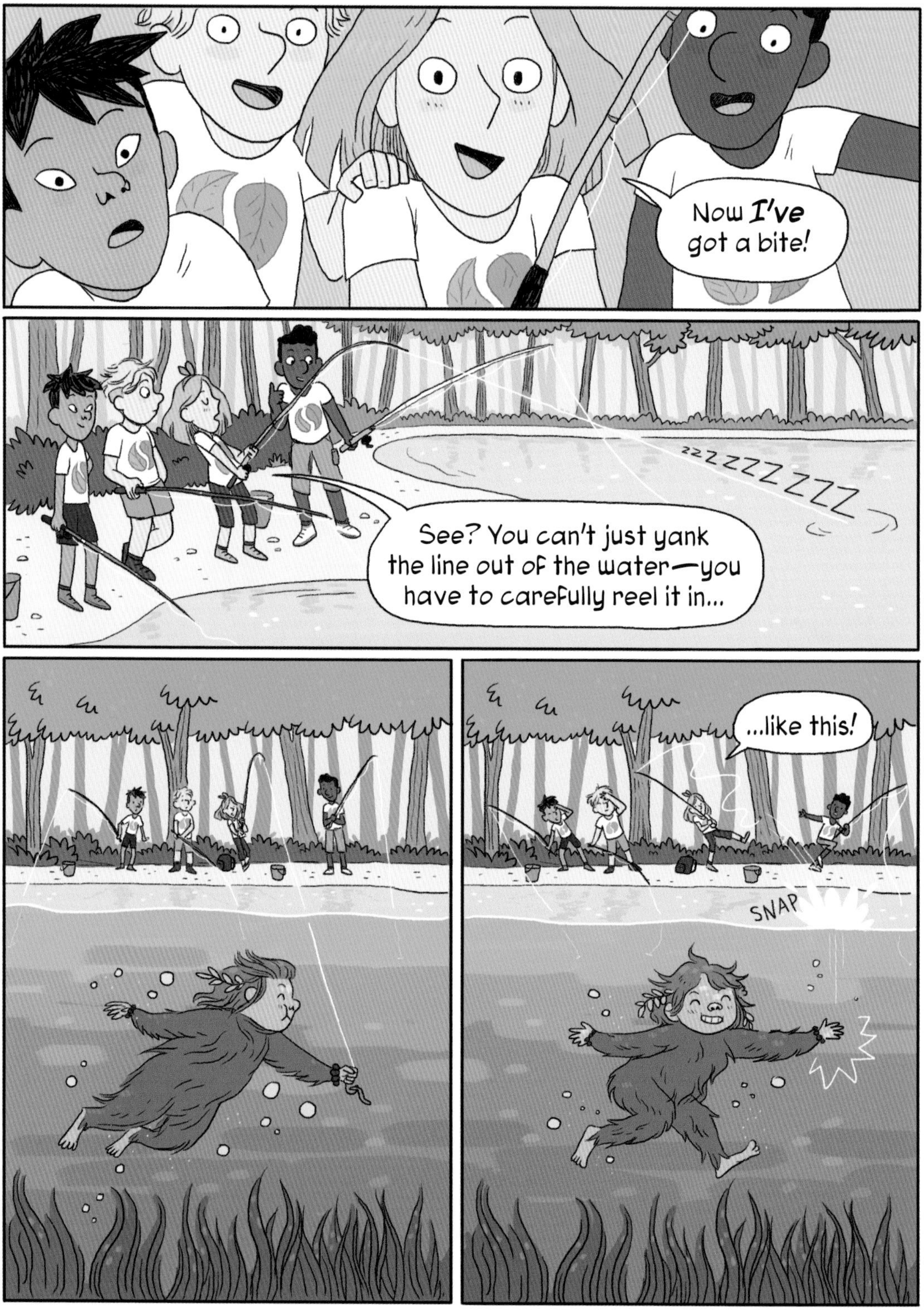
Now I've got a bite!
See? You can't just yank the line out of the water—you have to carefully reel it in...
zzZZZZZZZ
...like this!
SNAP

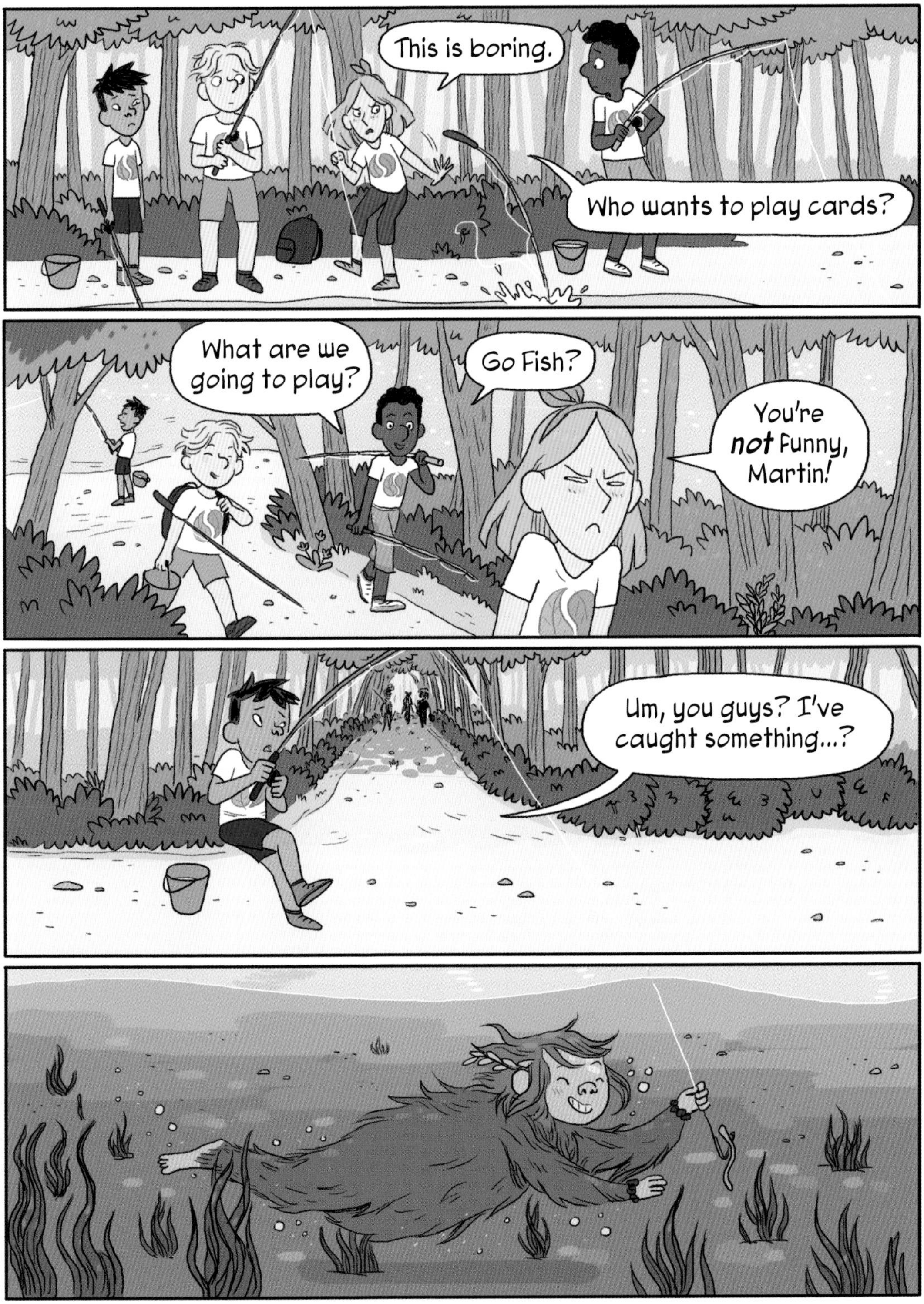

This is boring.
Who wants to play cards?
What are we going to play?
Go Fish?
You're **not** funny, Martin!
Um, you guys? I've caught something...?

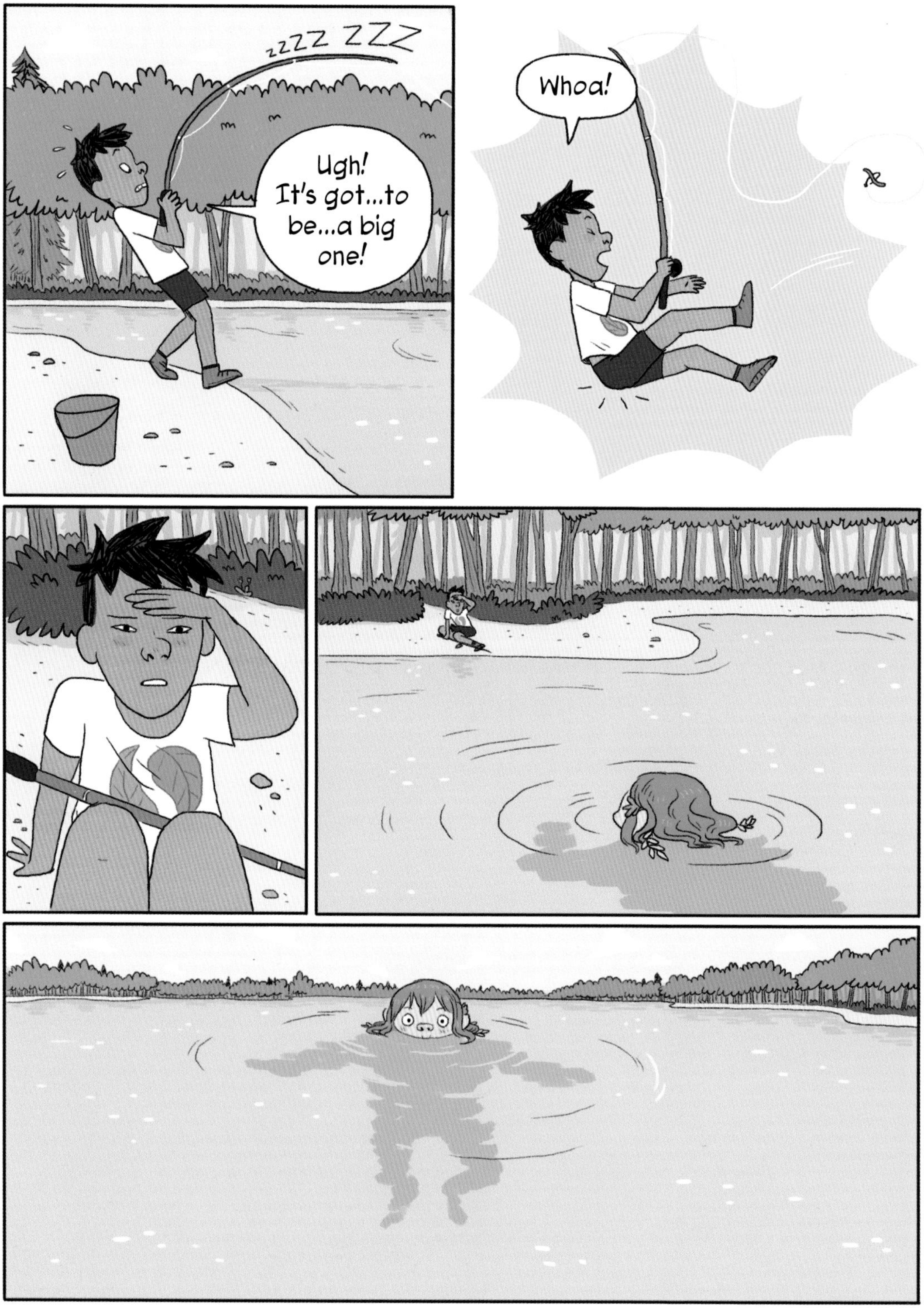
zzZZ ZZZ
Ugh! It's got...to be...a big one!
Whoa!

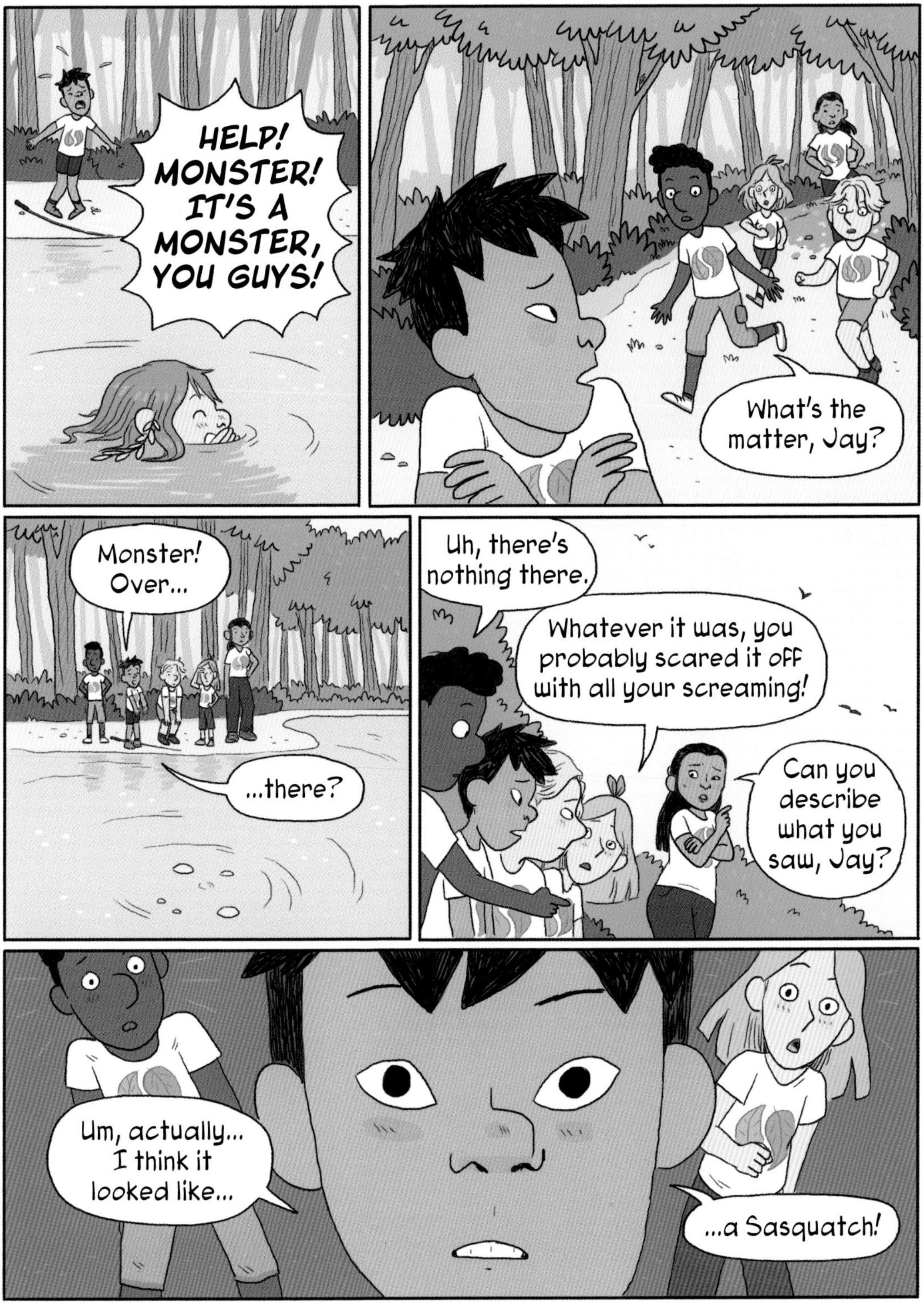
HELP! MONSTER! IT'S A MONSTER, YOU GUYS!
What's the matter, Jay?
Monster! Over...
...there?
Uh, there's nothing there.
Whatever it was, you probably scared it off with all your screaming!
Can you describe what you saw, Jay?
Um, actually... I think it looked like...
...a Sasquatch!

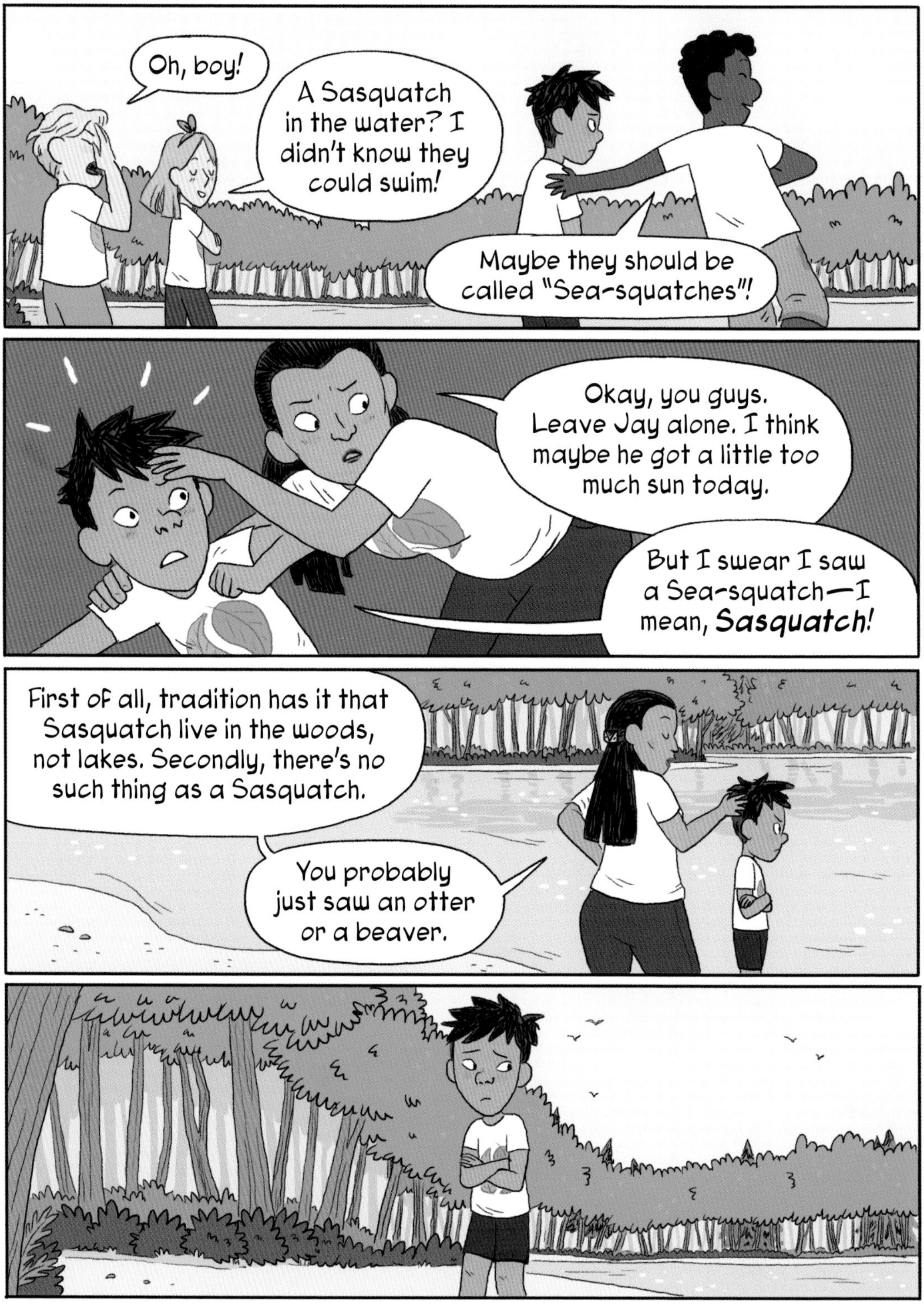
Oh, boy!
A Sasquatch in the water? I didn't know they could swim!
Maybe they should be called "Sea-squatches"!
Okay, you guys. Leave Jay alone. I think maybe he got a little too much sun today.
But I swear I saw a Sea-squatch—I mean, **Sasquatch**!
First of all, tradition has it that Sasquatch live in the woods, not lakes. Secondly, there's no such thing as a Sasquatch.
You probably just saw an otter or a beaver.

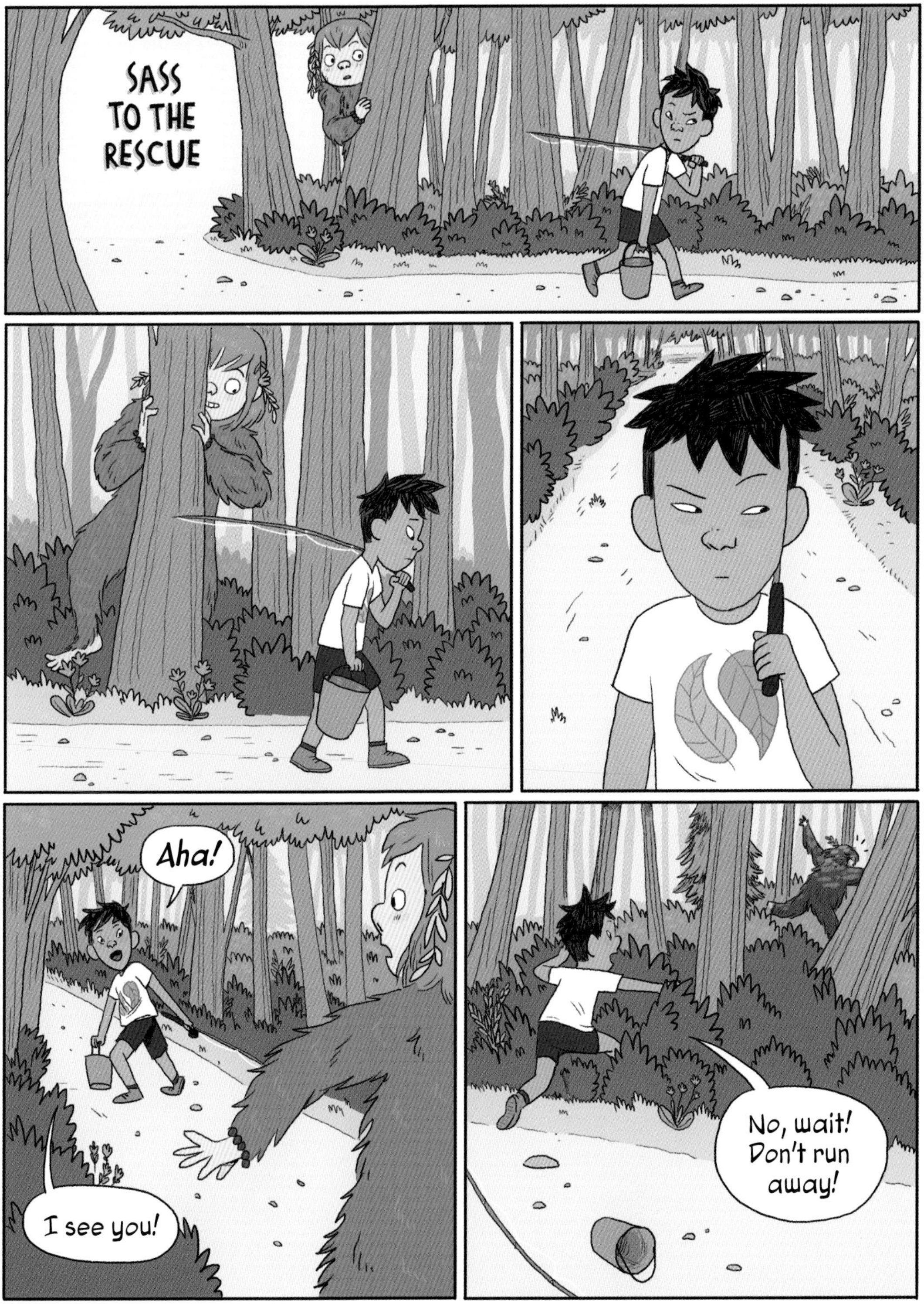

SASS TO THE RESCUE
Aha!
I see you!
No, wait! Don't run away!

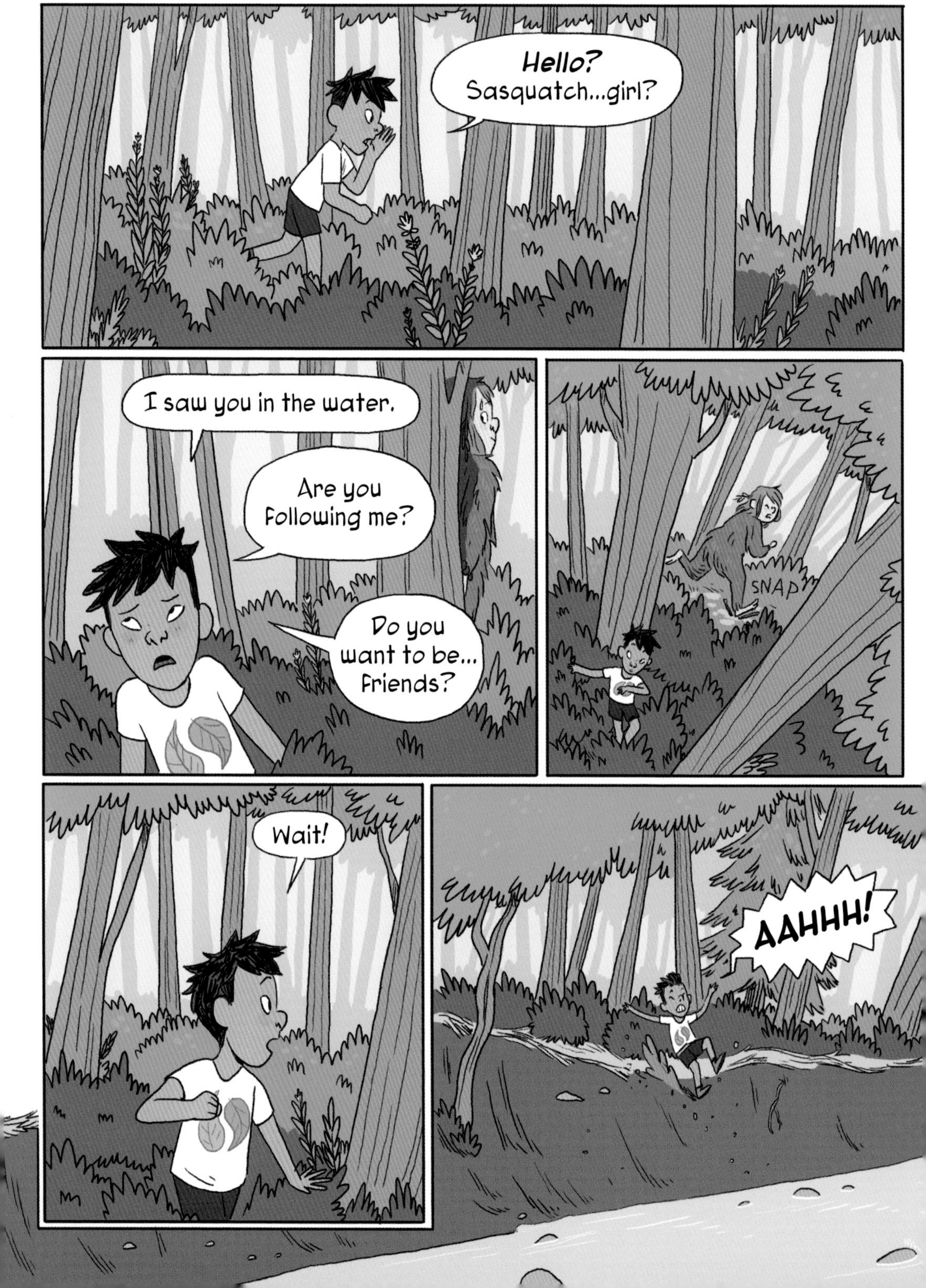
Hello? Sasquatch...girl?
I saw you in the water.
Are you following me?
Do you want to be... friends?
SNAP
Wait!
AAHHH!

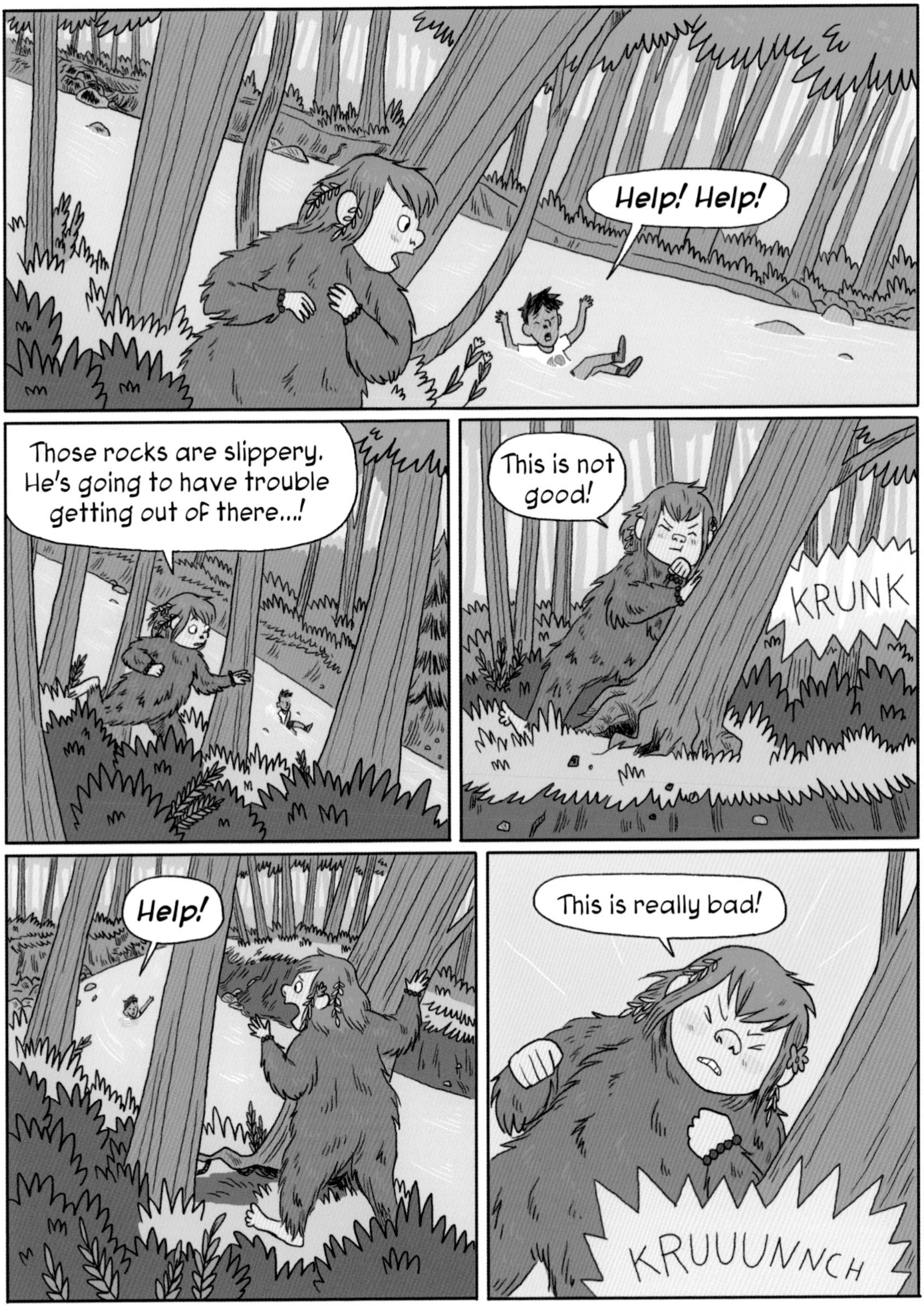
Help! Help!
Those rocks are slippery. He's going to have trouble getting out of there...!
This is not good!
KRUNK
Help!
This is really bad!
KRUUUNNCH

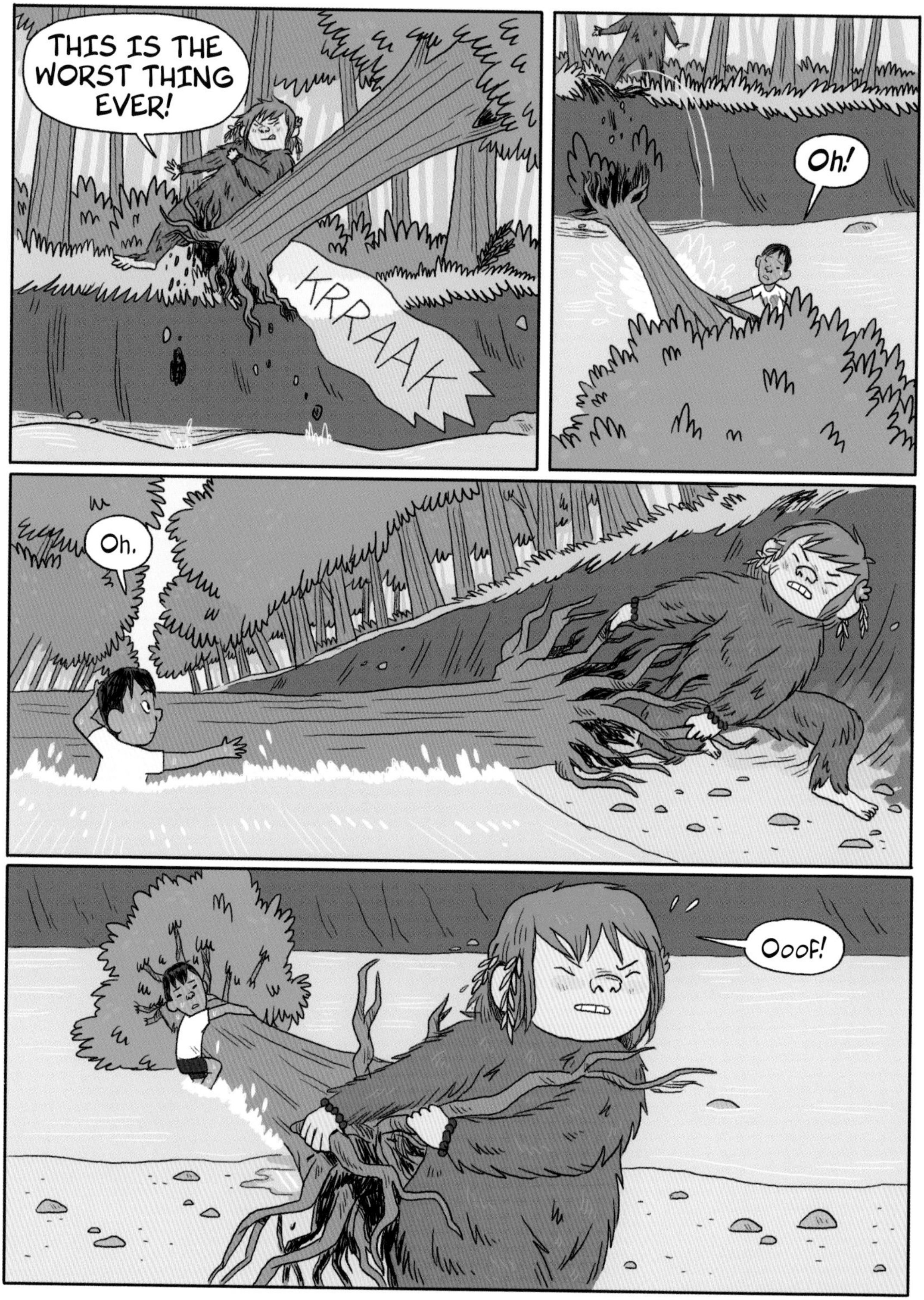
THIS IS THE WORST THING EVER!
KRRAAK
Oh!
Oh.
Ooof!

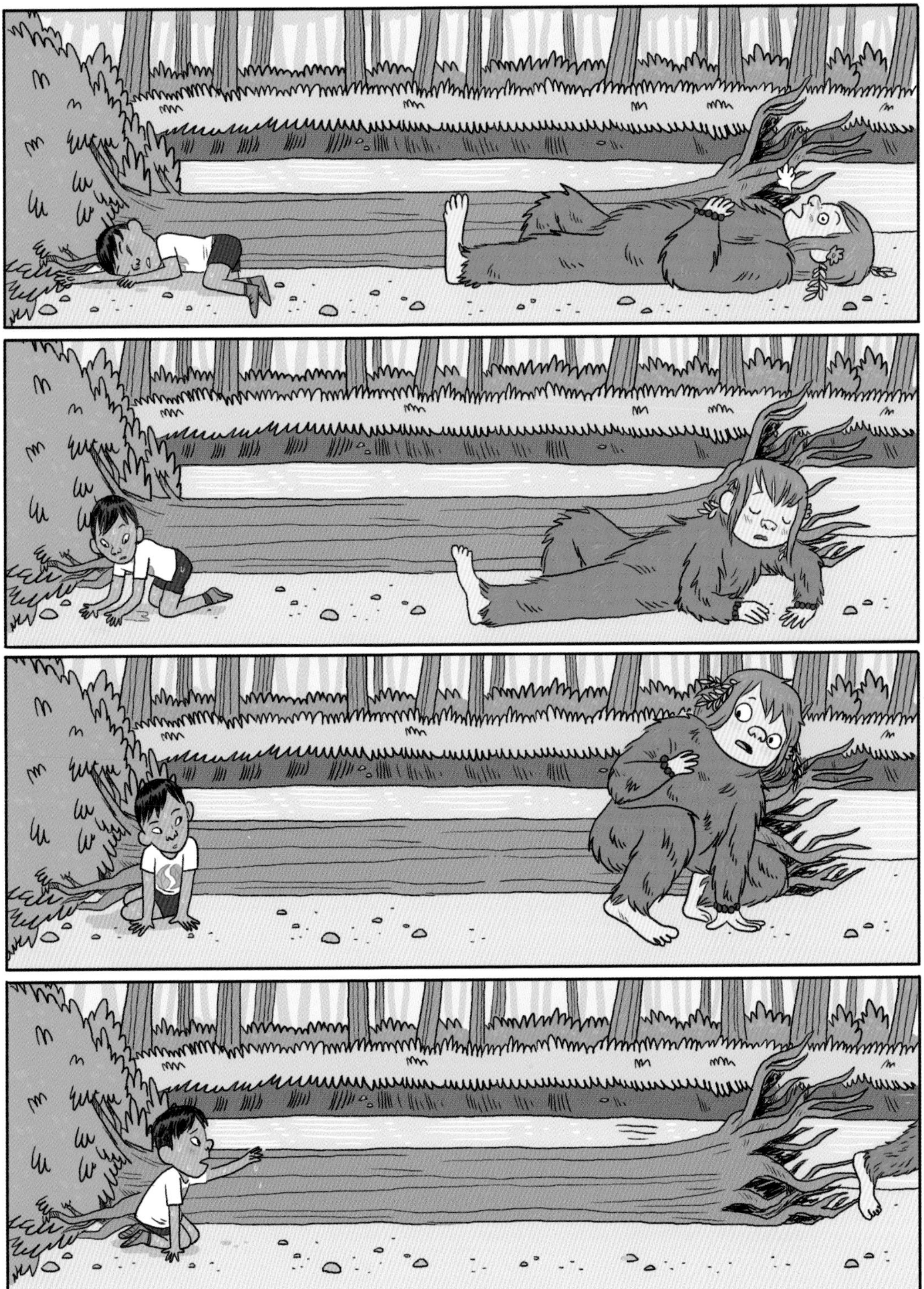

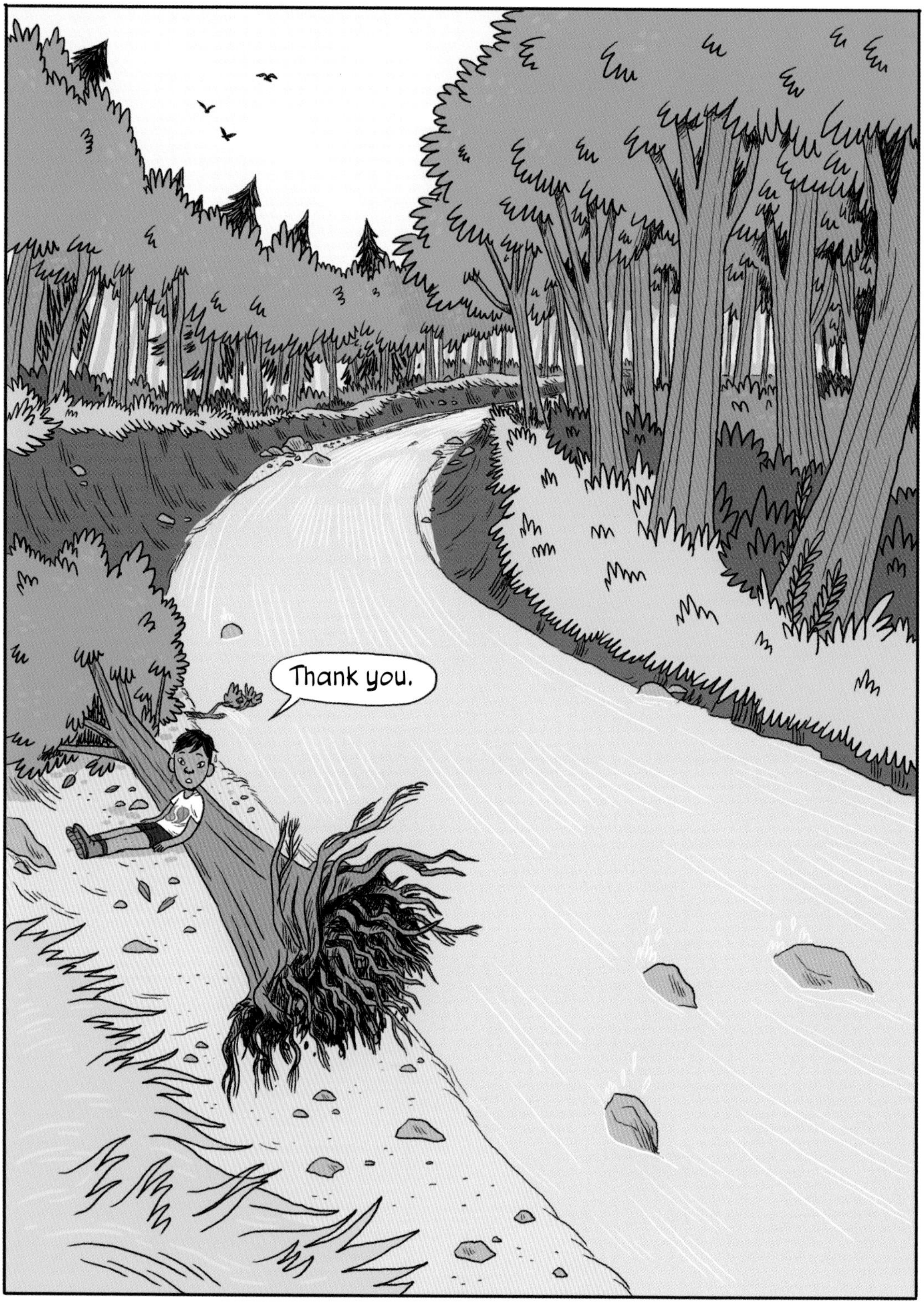
Thank you.

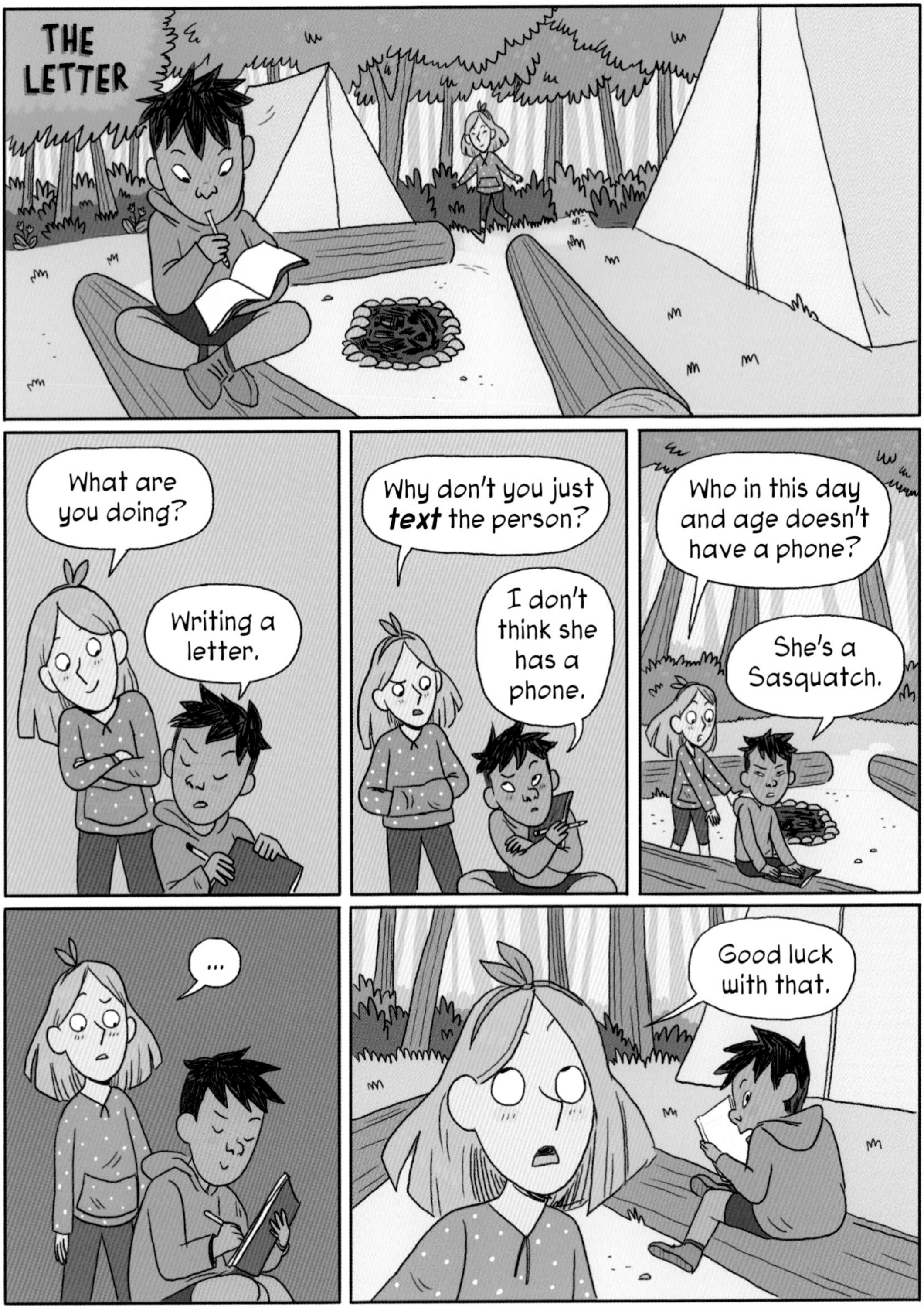
THE LETTER
What are you doing?
Writing a letter.
Why don't you just **text** the person?
I don't think she has a phone.
Who in this day and age doesn't have a phone?
She's a Sasquatch.
...
Good luck with that.

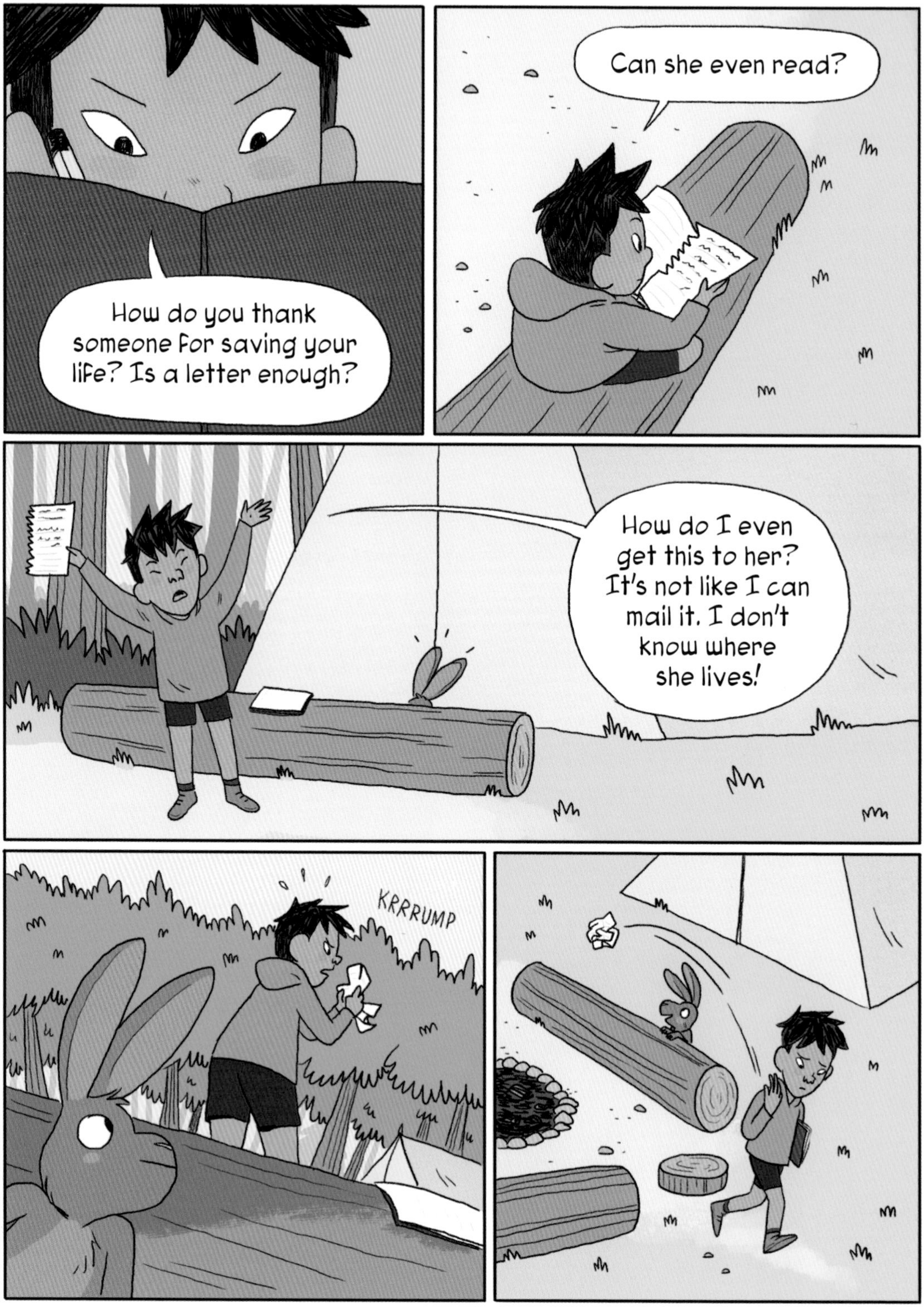
How do you thank someone for saving your life? Is a letter enough?
Can she even read?
How do I even get this to her? It's not like I can mail it. I don't know where she lives!
KRRRUMP

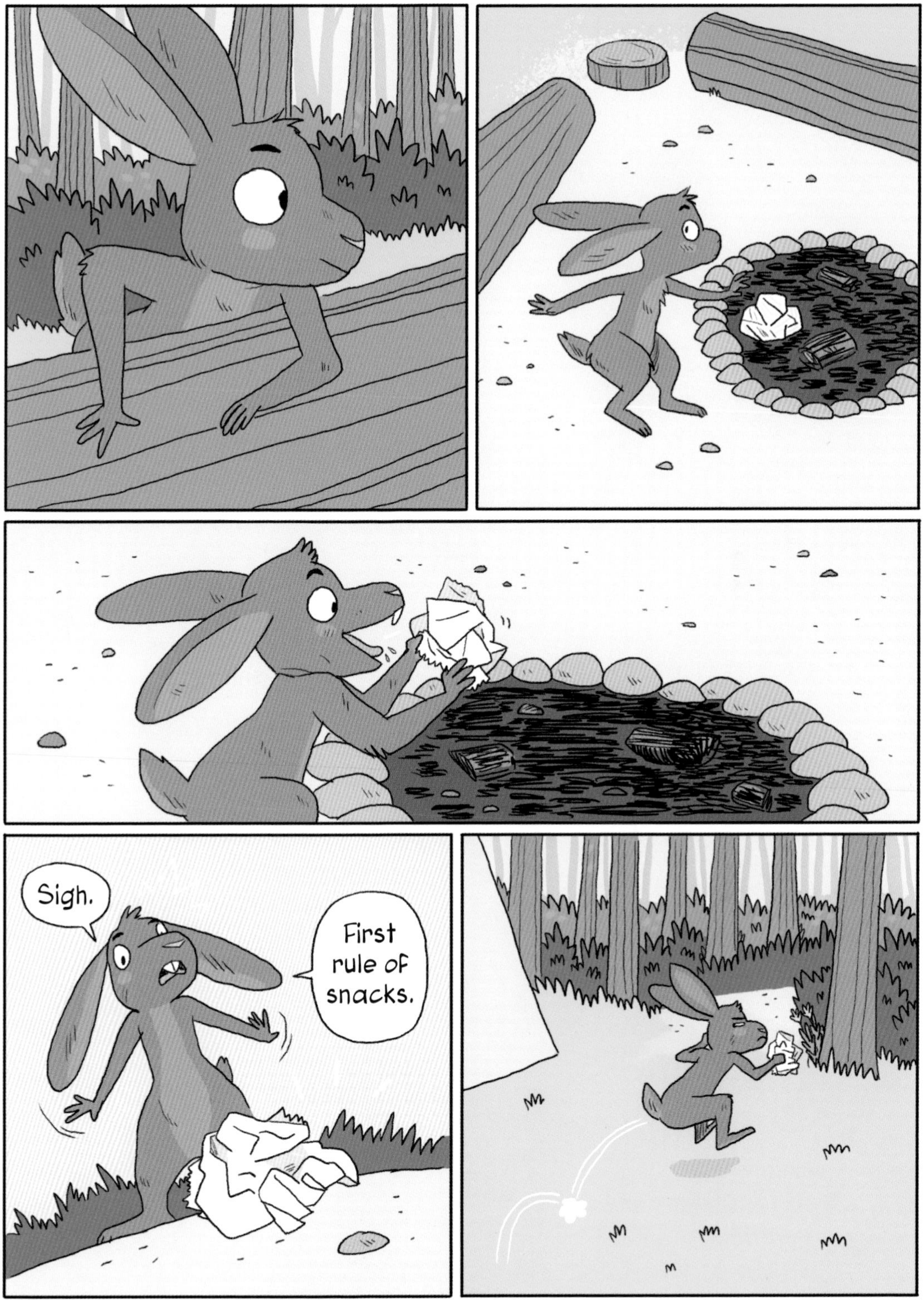
Sigh.
First rule of snacks.

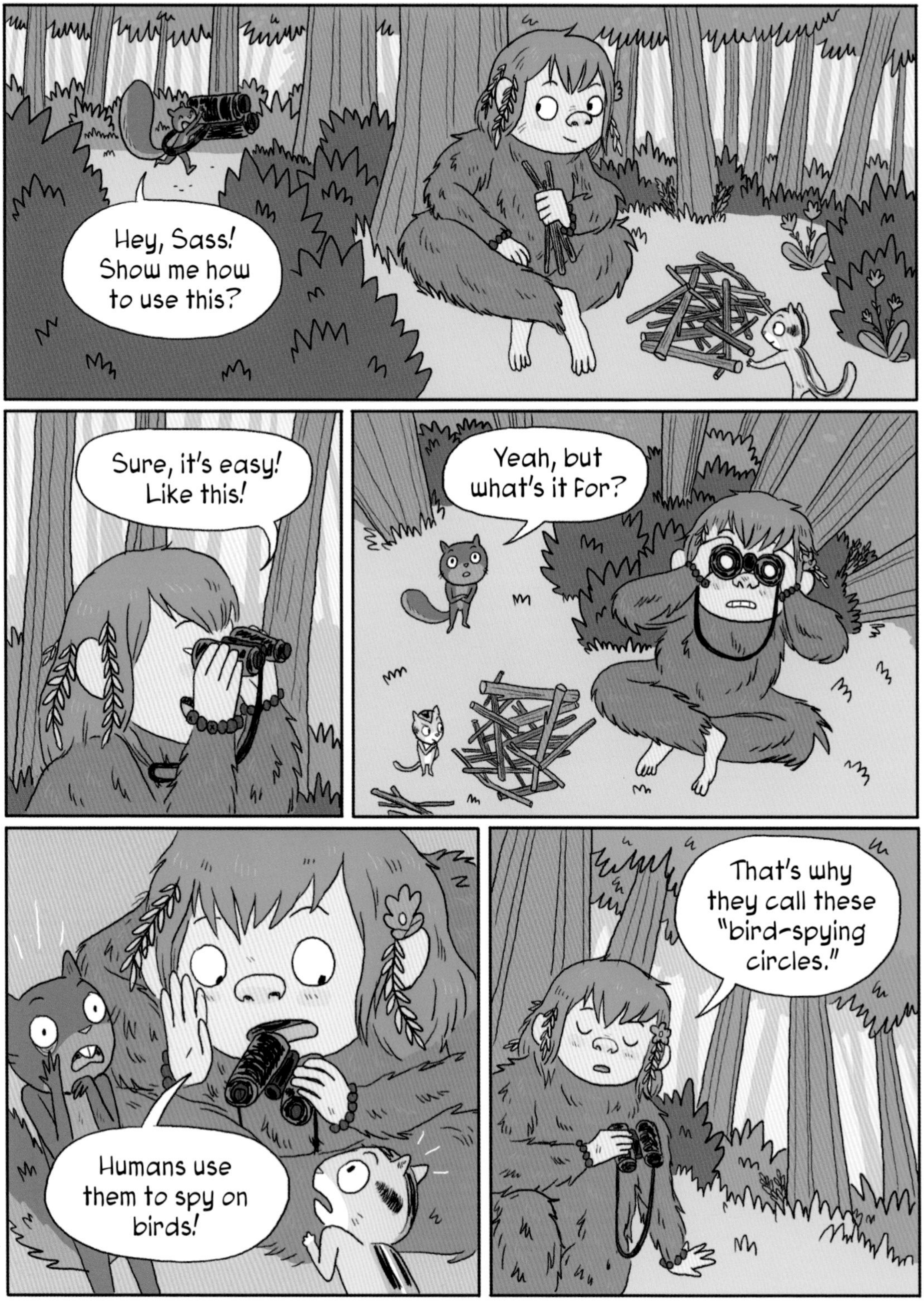
Hey, Sass! Show me how to use this?
Sure, it's easy! Like this!
Yeah, but what's it for?
Humans use them to spy on birds!
That's why they call these "bird-spying circles."

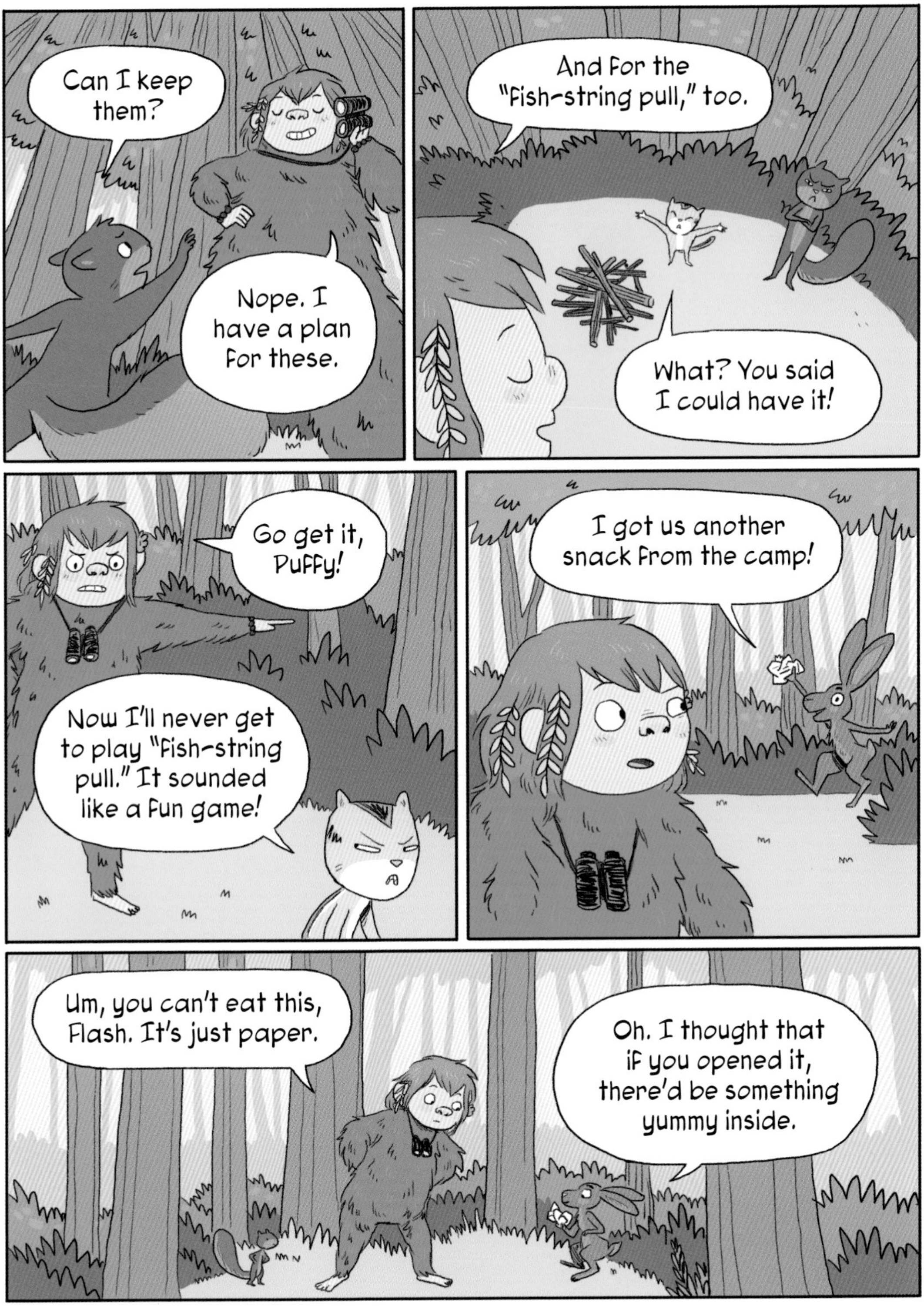

Can I keep them?
Nope. I have a plan for these.
And for the "fish-string pull," too.
What? You said I could have it!
Go get it, Puffy!
Now I'll never get to play "fish-string pull." It sounded like a fun game!
I got us another snack from the camp!
Um, you can't eat this, Flash. It's just paper.
Oh. I thought that if you opened it, there'd be something yummy inside.

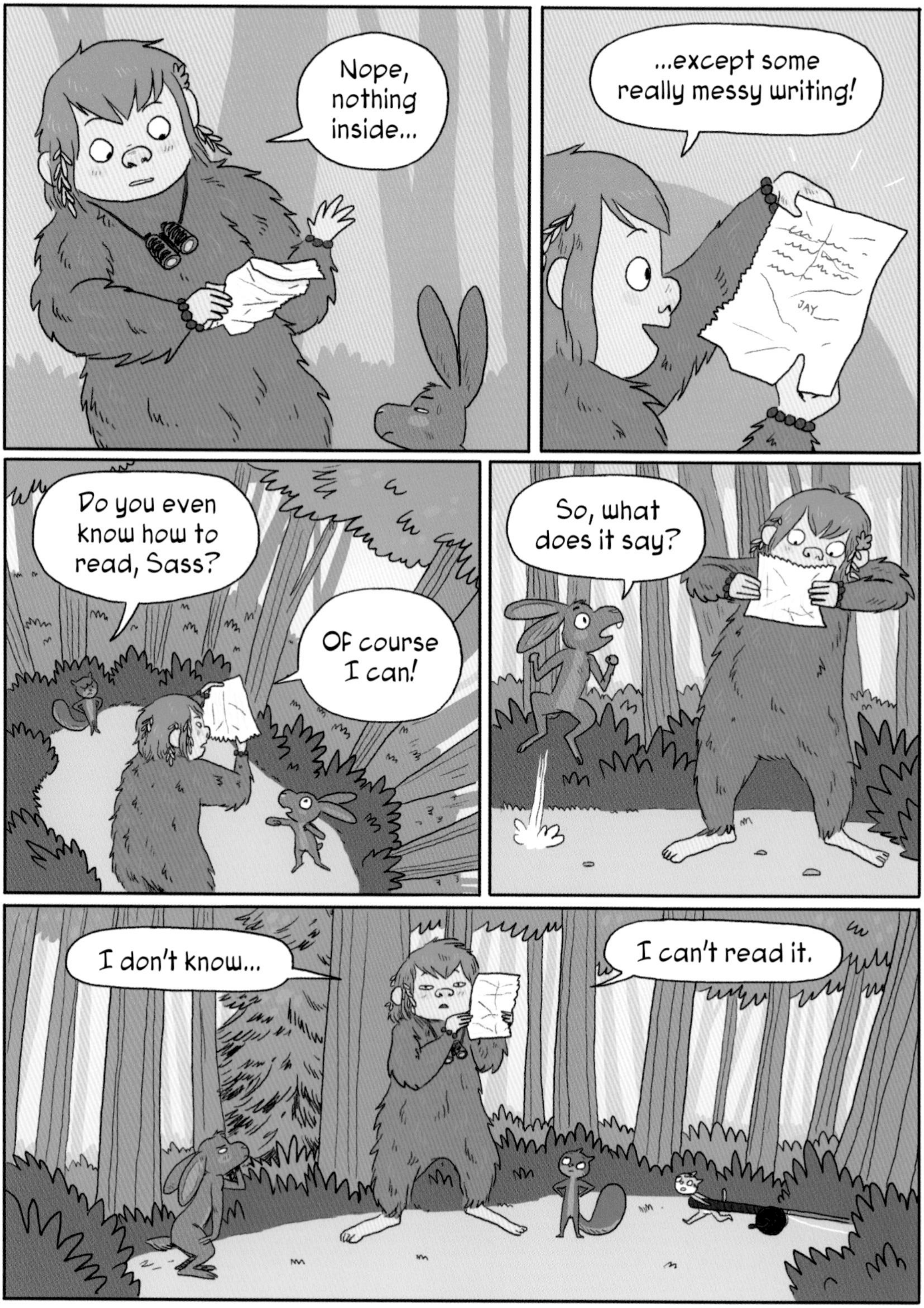
Nope, nothing inside...
...except some really messy writing!
JAY
Do you even know how to read, Sass?
Of course I can!
So, what does it say?
I don't know...
I can't read it.

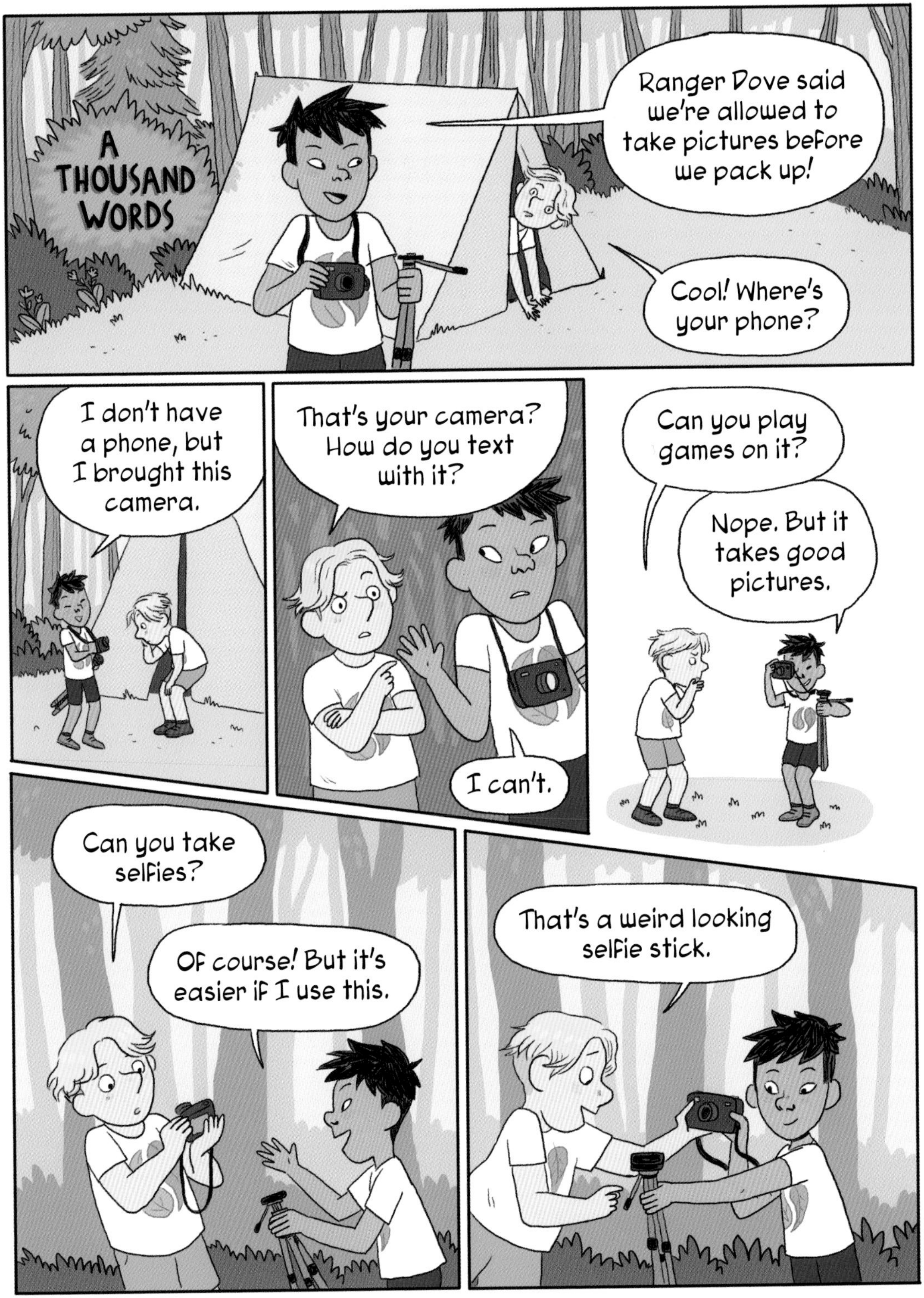
A THOUSAND WORDS
Ranger Dove said we're allowed to take pictures before we pack up!
Cool! Where's your phone?
I don't have a phone, but I brought this camera.
That's your camera? How do you text with it?
I can't.
Can you play games on it?
Nope. But it takes good pictures.
Can you take selfies?
Of course! But it's easier if I use this.
That's a weird looking selfie stick.

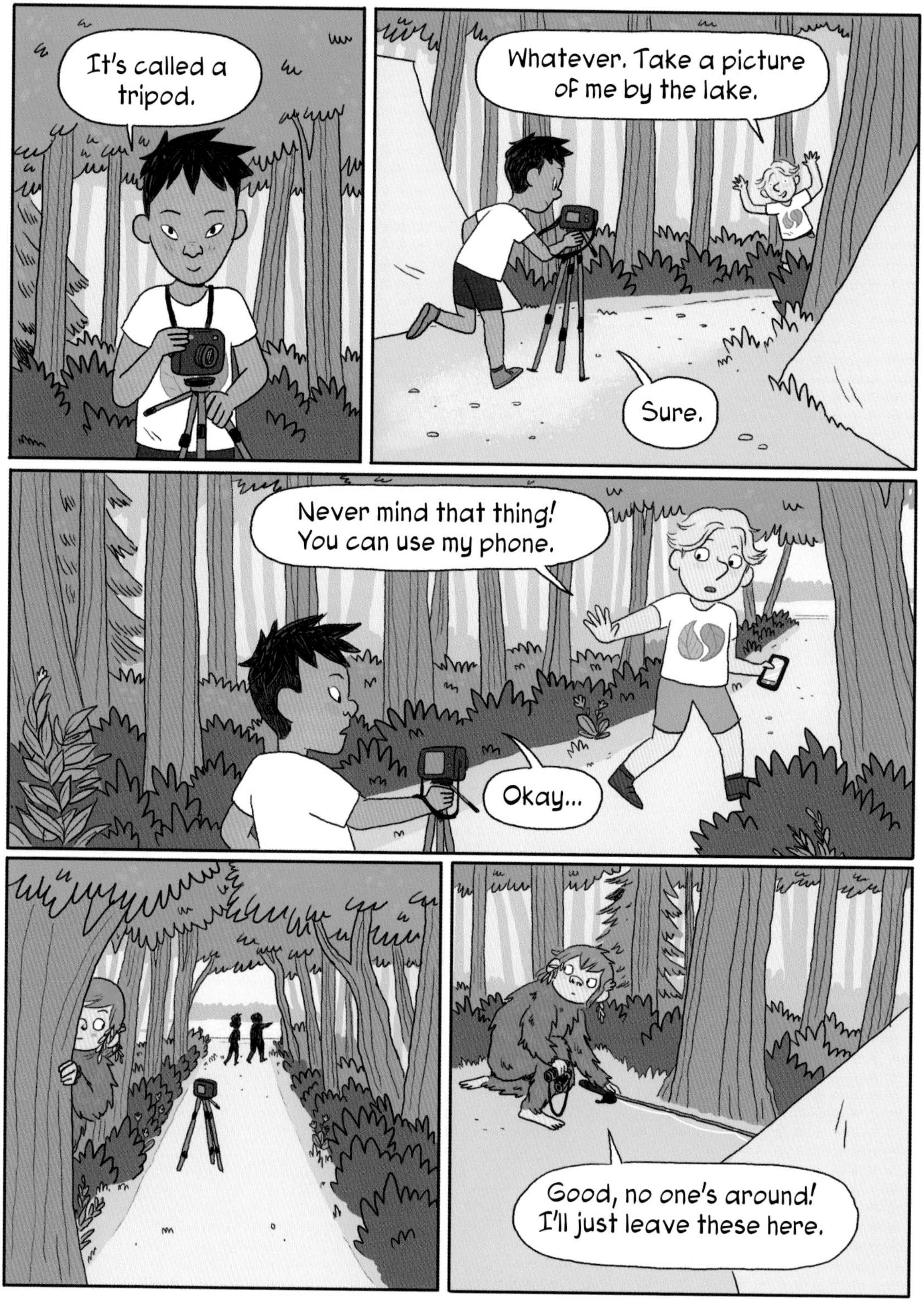
It's called a tripod.
Whatever. Take a picture of me by the lake.
Sure.
Never mind that thing! You can use my phone.
Okay...
Good, no one's around! I'll just leave these here.

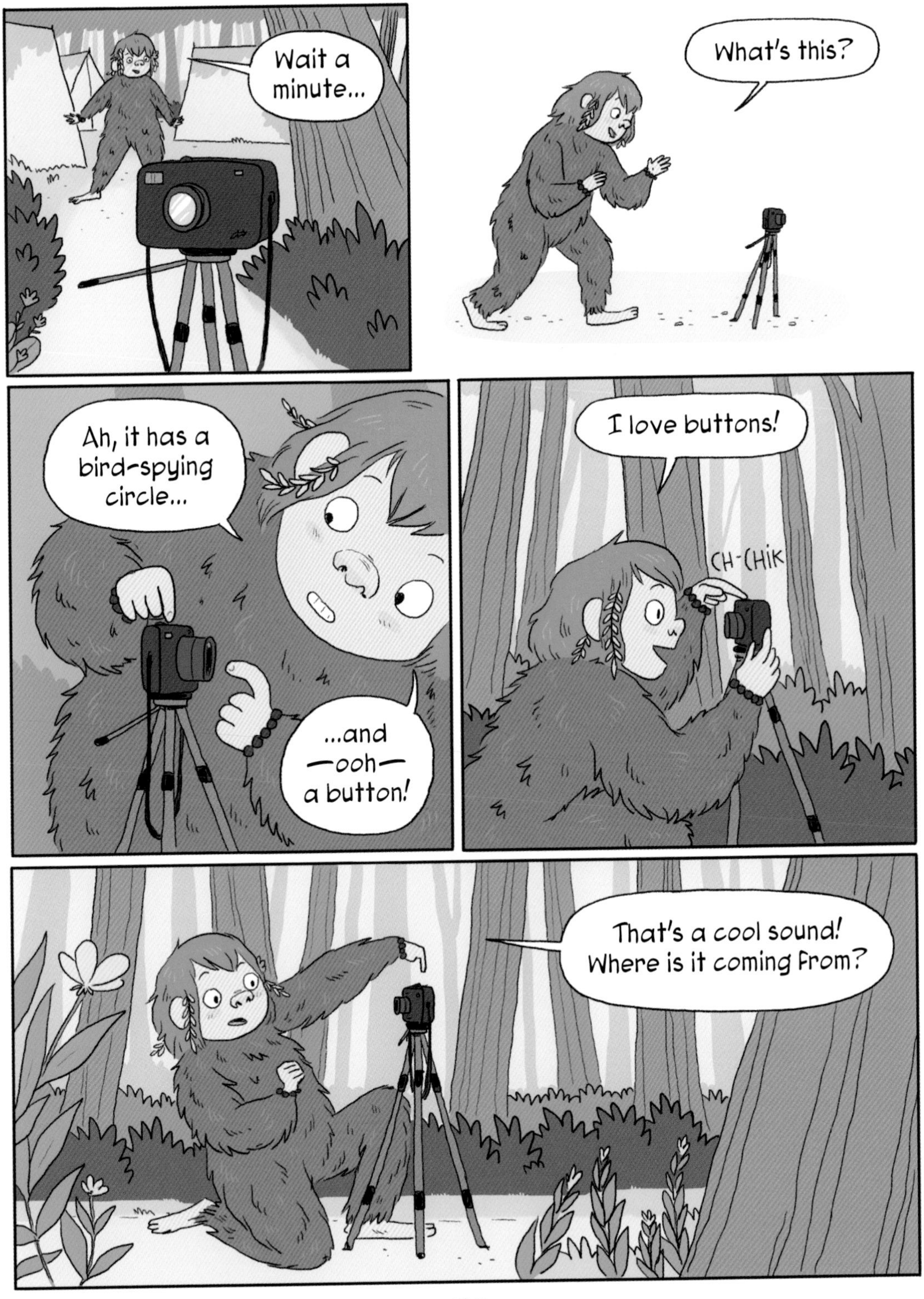
Wait a minute...
What's this?
Ah, it has a bird-spying circle...
...and —ooh— a button!
I love buttons!
CH-CHIK
That's a cool sound! Where is it coming from?

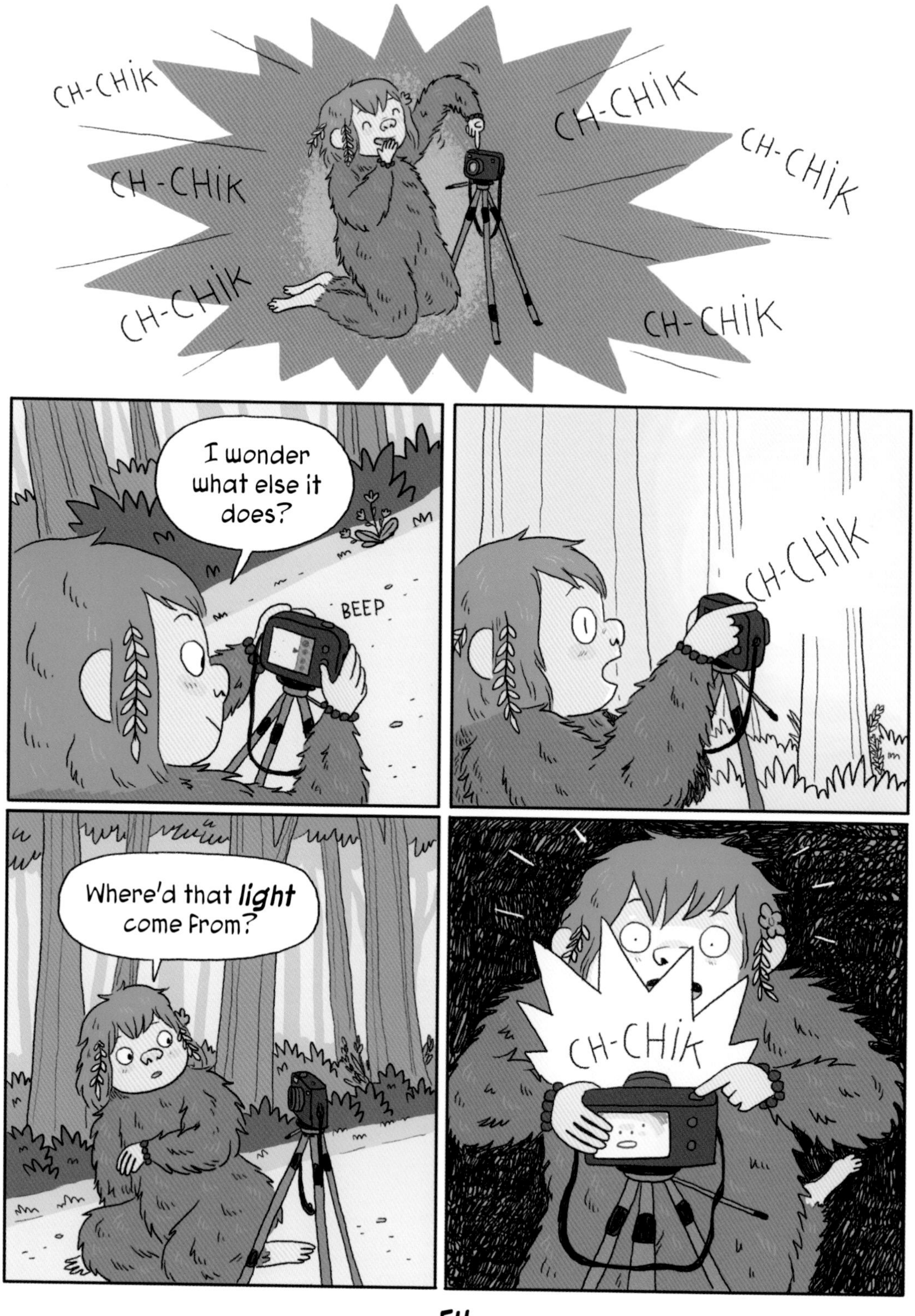
CH-CHIK
CH-CHIK
CH-CHIK
CH-CHIK
CH-CHIK
CH-CHIK
I wonder what else it does?
BEEP
CH-CHIK
Where'd that **light** come from?
CH-CHIK

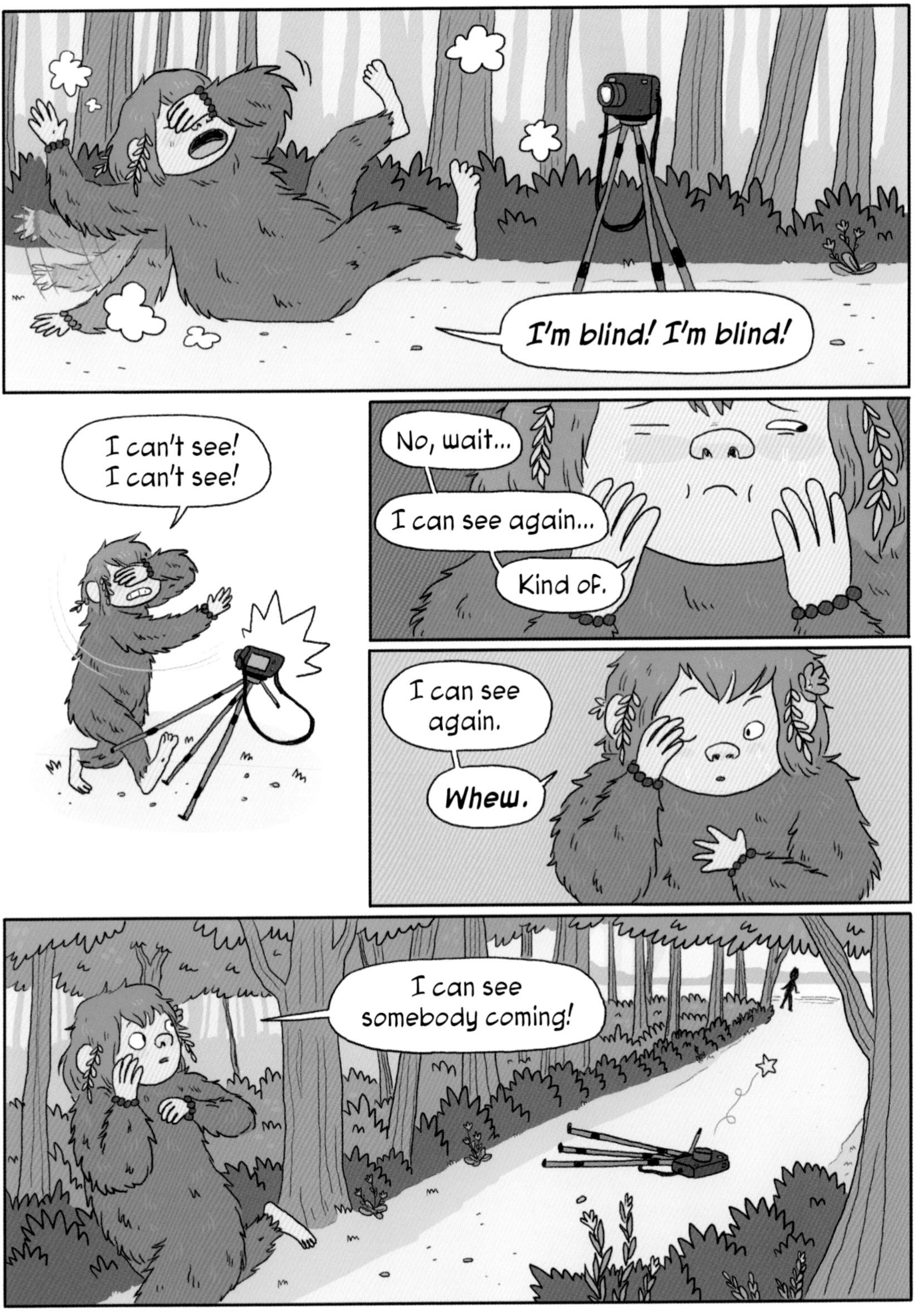
I'm blind! I'm blind!
I can't see! I can't see!
No, wait...
I can see again...
Kind of.
I can see again.
Whew.
I can see somebody coming!

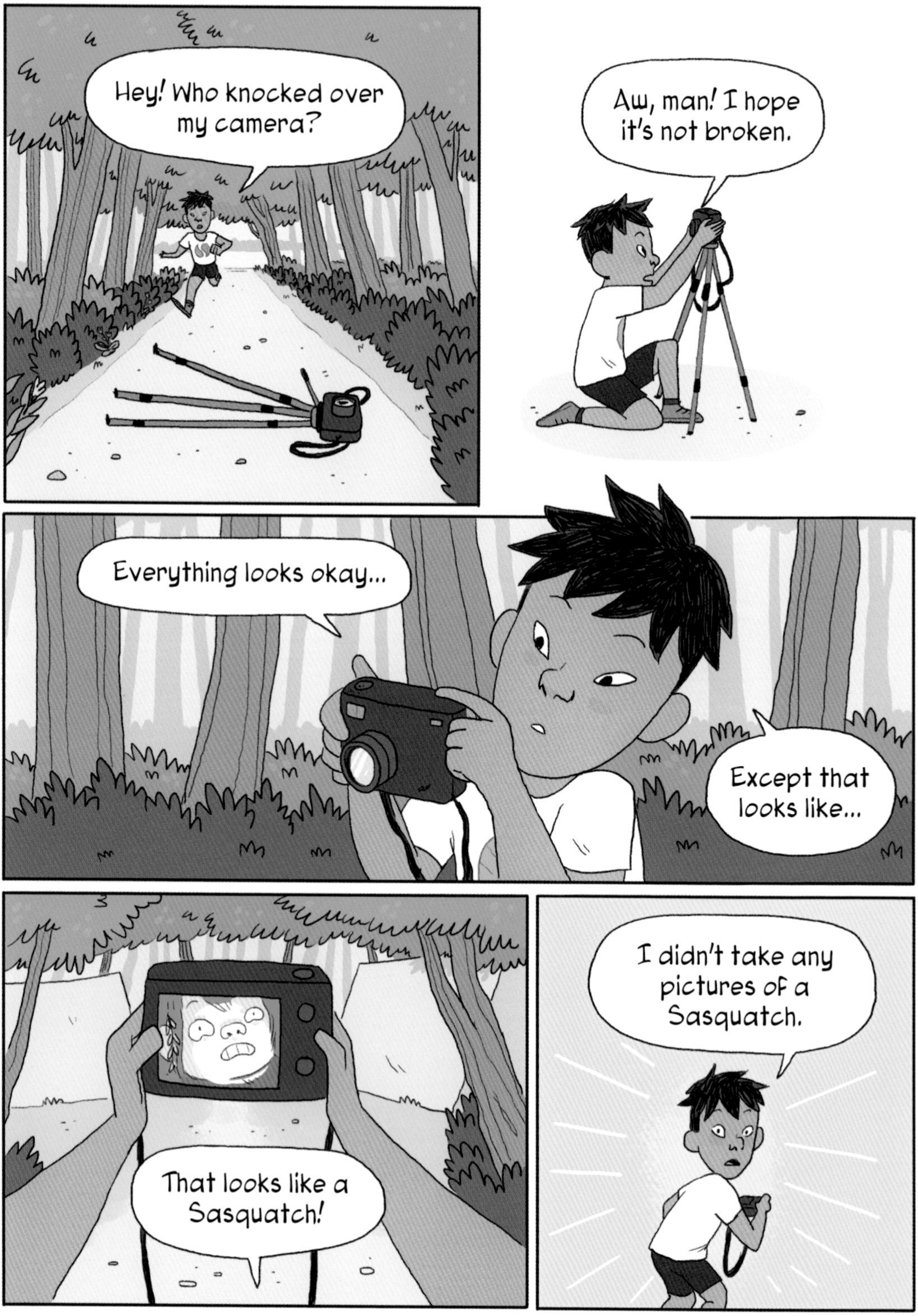
Hey! Who knocked over my camera?
Aw, man! I hope it's not broken.
Everything looks okay...
Except that looks like...
That looks like a Sasquatch!
I didn't take any pictures of a Sasquatch.

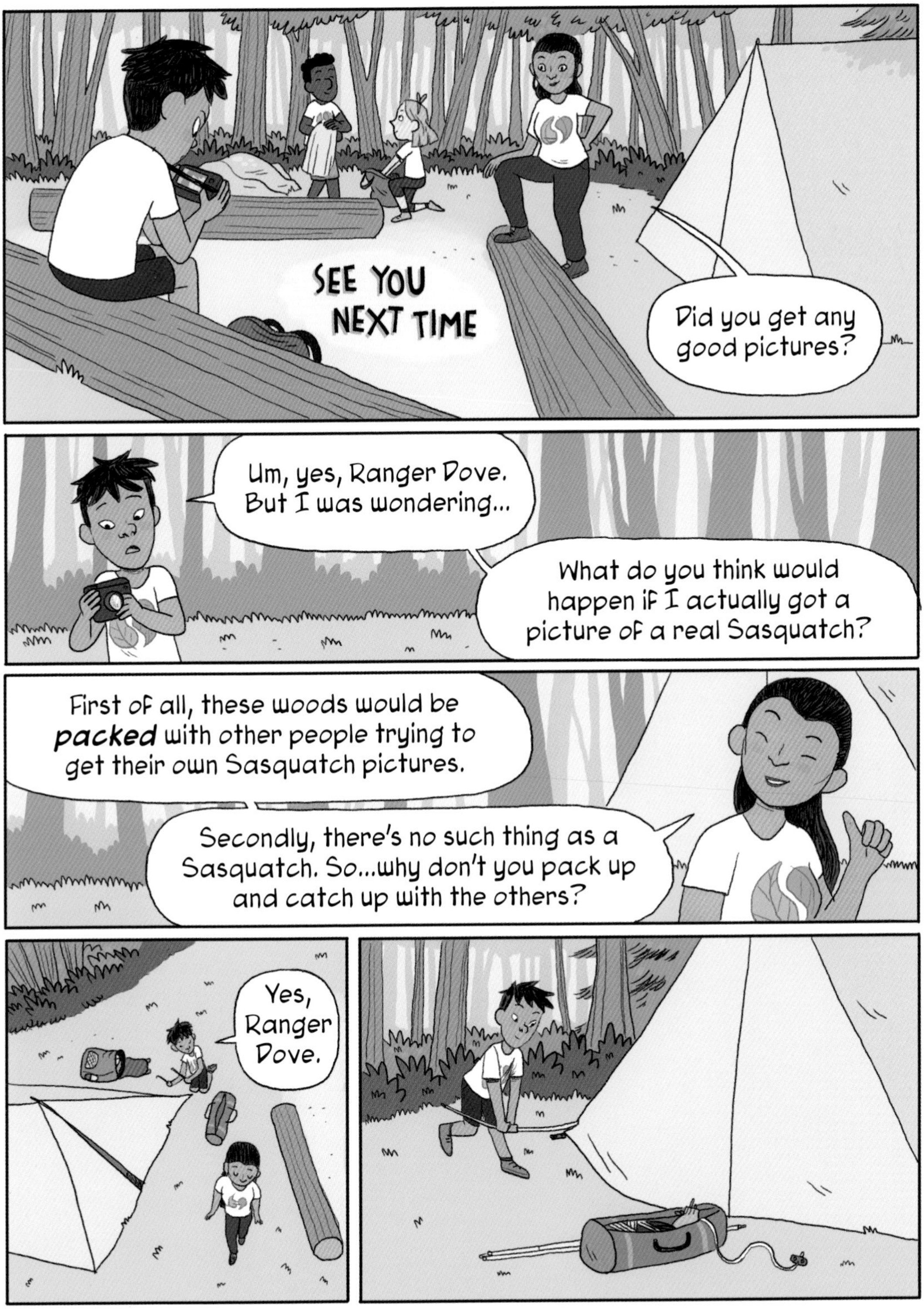
SEE YOU NEXT TIME
Did you get any good pictures?
Um, yes, Ranger Dove. But I was wondering...
What do you think would happen if I actually got a picture of a real Sasquatch?
First of all, these woods would be **packed** with other people trying to get their own Sasquatch pictures.
Secondly, there's no such thing as a Sasquatch. So...why don't you pack up and catch up with the others?
Yes, Ranger Dove.

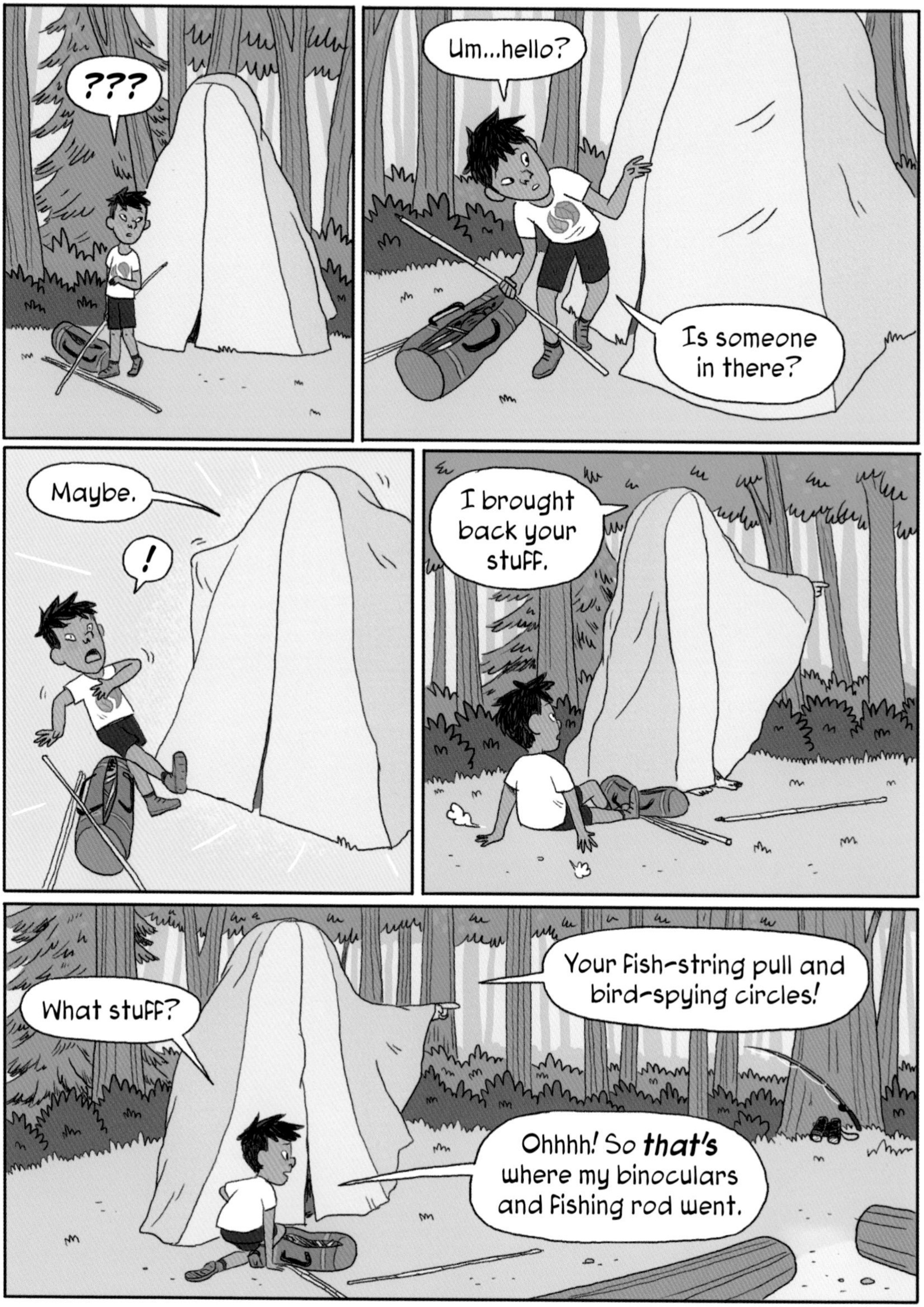
???
Um...hello?
Is someone in there?
Maybe.
!
I brought back your stuff.
What stuff?
Your fish-string pull and bird-spying circles!
Ohhhh! So **that's** where my binoculars and fishing rod went.

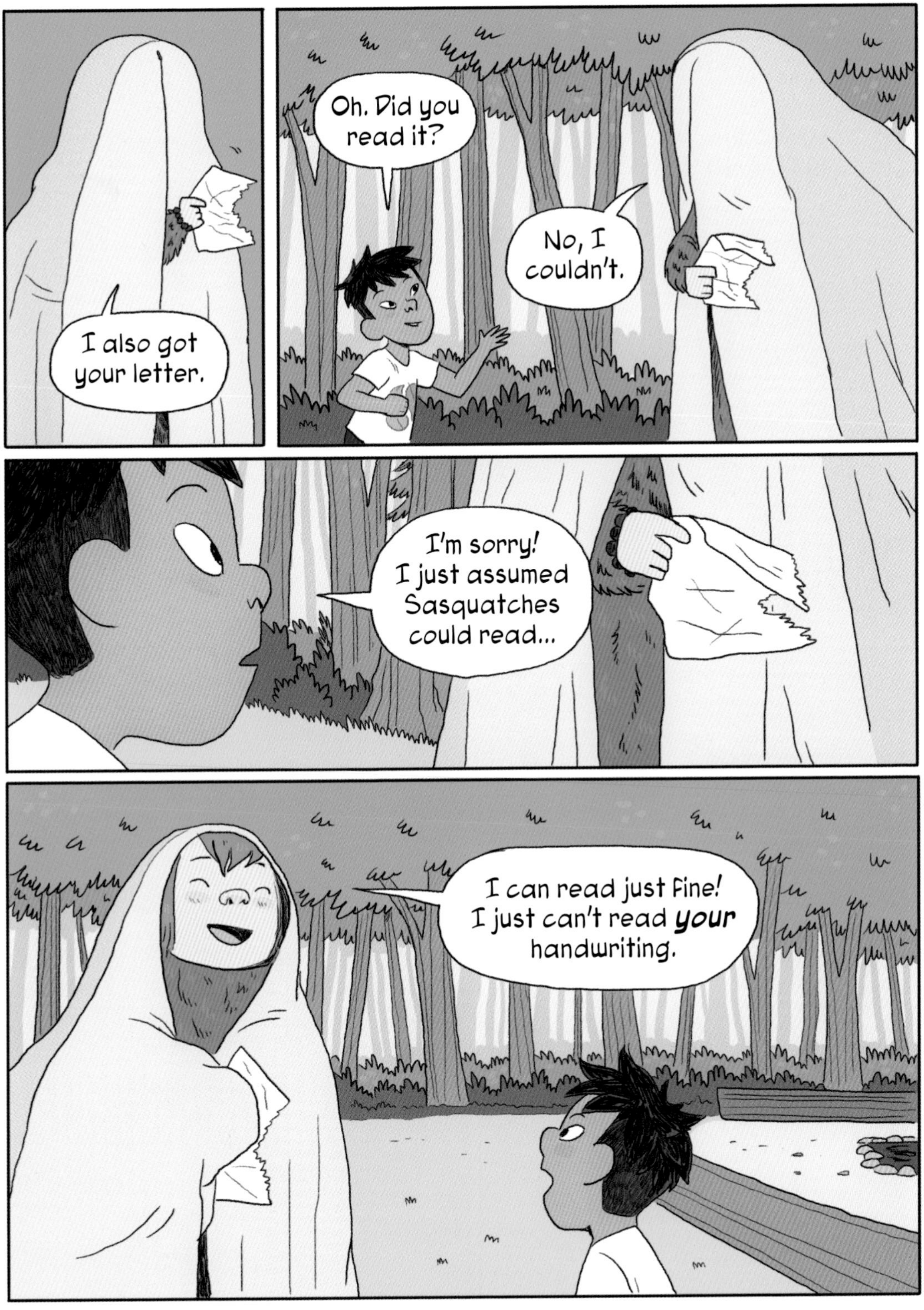
I also got your letter.
Oh. Did you read it?
No, I couldn't.
I'm sorry! I just assumed Sasquatches could read...
I can read just fine! I just can't read *your* handwriting.

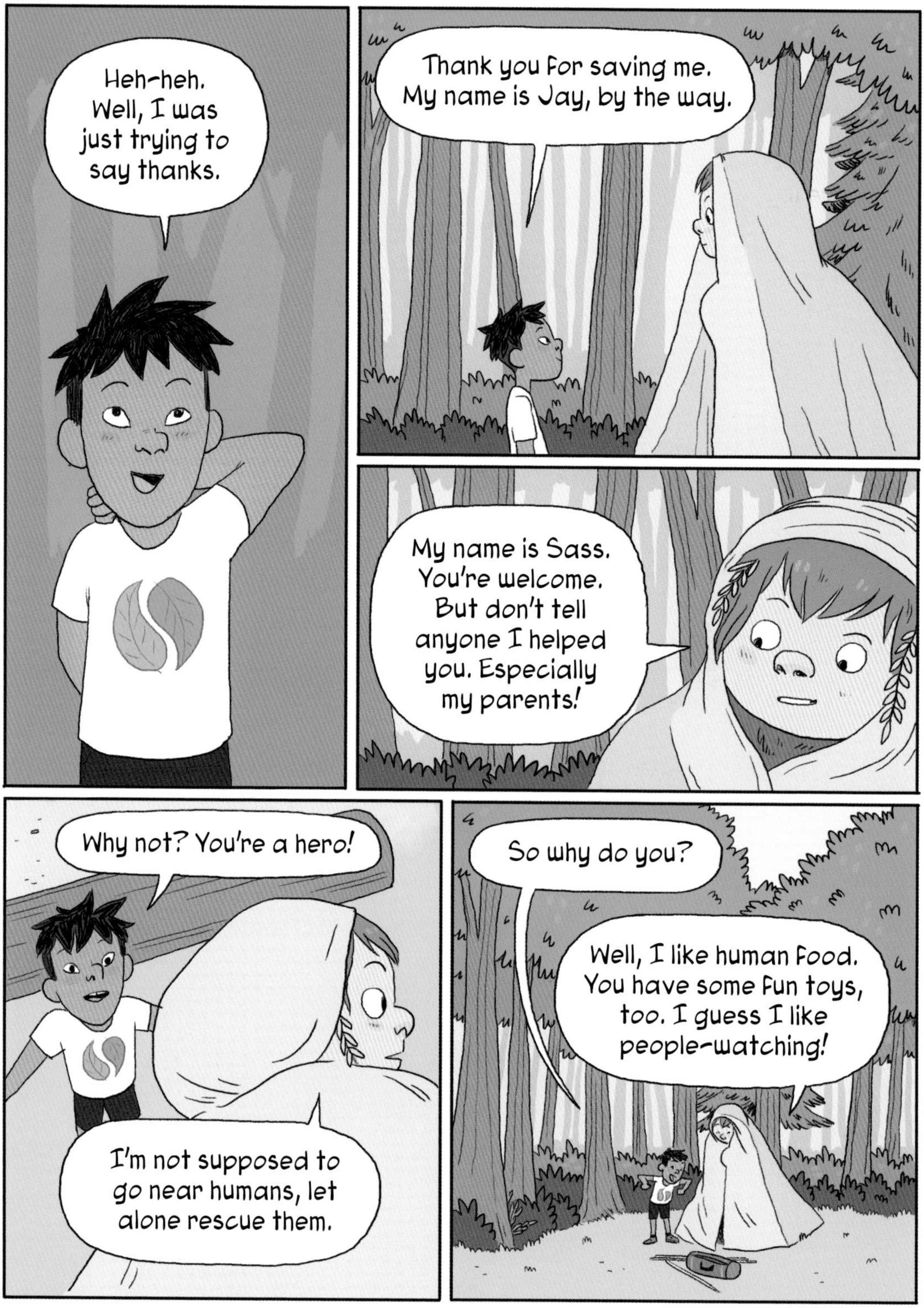
Heh-heh. Well, I was just trying to say thanks.
Thank you for saving me. My name is Jay, by the way.
My name is Sass. You're welcome. But don't tell anyone I helped you. Especially my parents!
Why not? You're a hero!
I'm not supposed to go near humans, let alone rescue them.
So why do you?
Well, I like human food. You have some fun toys, too. I guess I like people-watching!

Hey, I have an idea! You can have my binoculars.

They're good for looking at things from a distance.

I know that! Like birds—duh!

Or people! So you can do all the people-watching you want without getting close!

Wow, thanks! I think my parents will like that.

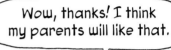

You're going to *tell* them you spoke to a human today?

Yeah. Probably not a good idea.

Are *you* going to tell anyone that you spoke to a Sasquatch?

I'd love to but they wouldn't believe me.

Anyway, it's probably better for you that no one knows you're real.

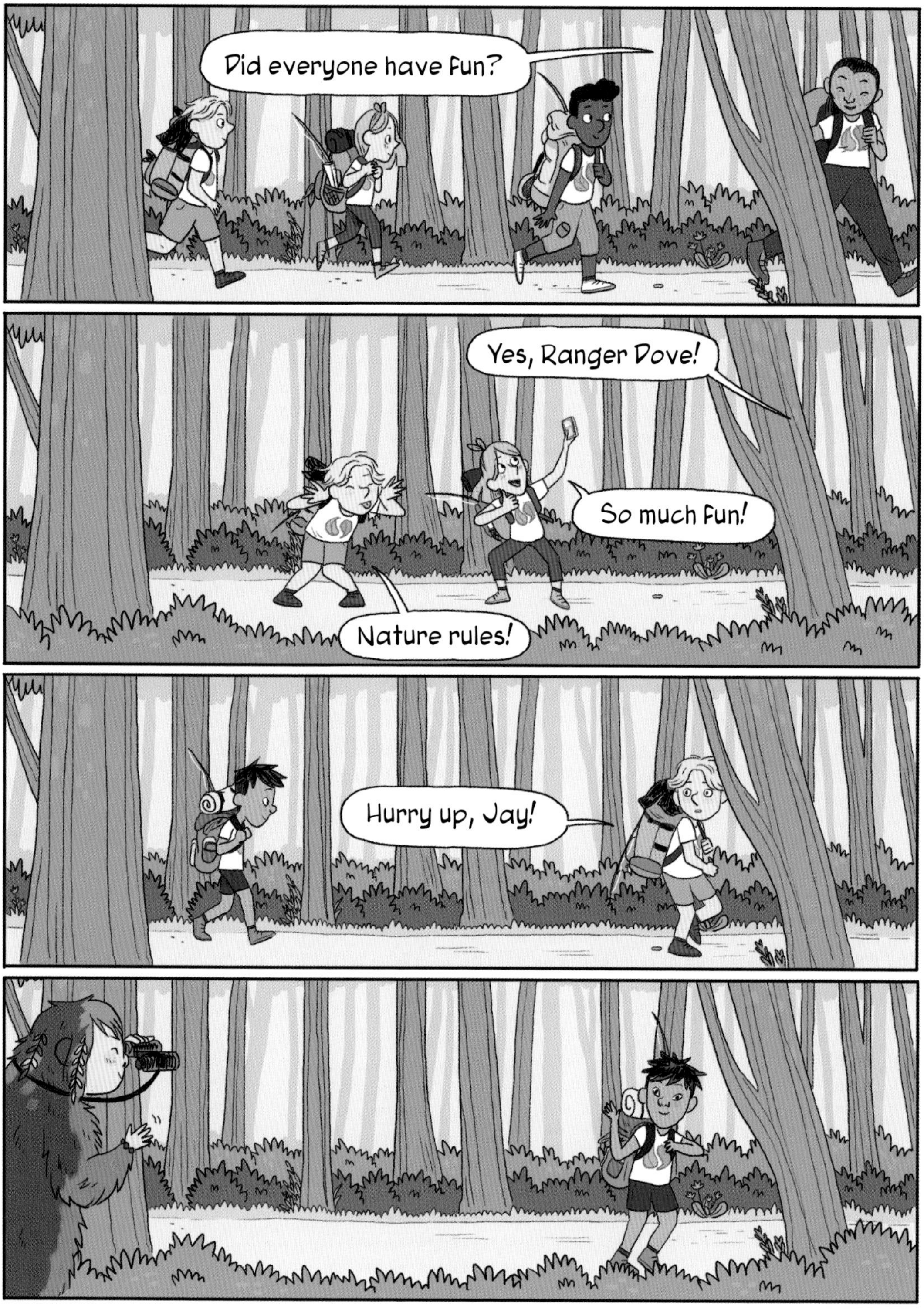
Did everyone have fun?
Yes, Ranger Dove!
So much fun!
Nature rules!
Hurry up, Jay!

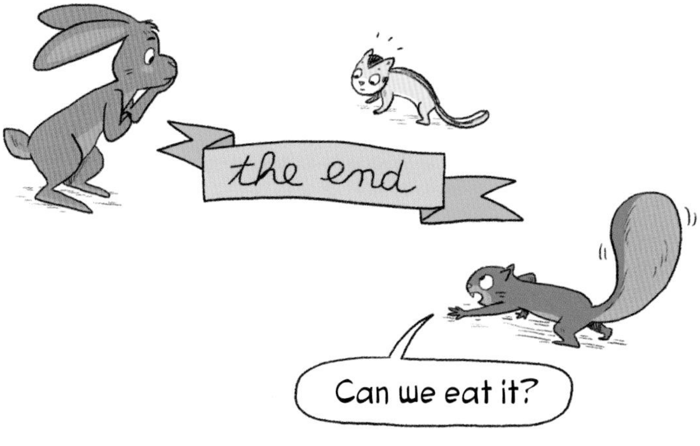
the end
Can we eat it?

First printing in paperback, 2022

Owlkids Books acknowledges the financial support of the Canada Council for the Arts, the Ontario Arts Council, the Government of Canada through the Canada Book Fund (CBF) and the Government of Ontario through the Ontario Creates Book Initiative for our publishing activities.

Published in Canada by
Owlkids Books Inc.
1 Eglinton Avenue East
Toronto, ON M4P 3A1

Published in the United States by
Owlkids Books Inc.
1700 Fourth Street
Berkeley, CA 94710

Library and Archives Canada Cataloguing in Publication

Title: How to spot a sasquatch / written by J. Torres ; illustrated by Aurélie Grand.
Names: Torres, J., 1969- author. | Grand, Aurélie, 1983- illustrator.
Identifiers: Canadiana 20210214724 | ISBN 9781771475273 (softcover)
Subjects: LCGFT: Graphic novels.
Classification: LCC PN6733.T67 J39 2022 | DDC j741.5/971—dc23

Library of Congress Control Number: 2017946102

The text is set in Blambot Pro.
Edited by: Karen Li and Debbie Rogosin
Designed by: Claudia Dávila

ONTARIO ARTS COUNCIL
CONSEIL DES ARTS DE L'ONTARIO
an Ontario government agency
un organisme du gouvernement de l'Ontario

Canada Council for the Arts
Conseil des Arts du Canada

Canadä

Manufactured in Shenzhen, China, in August 2021, by Printplus Limited
Job #S210700104

C D E F G H

Publisher of Chirp, Chickadee and OWL
www.owlkidsbooks.com

Owlkids Books is a division of bayard canada